William W. Newton

A Run through Russia

the story of a visit to Count Tolstoi

William W. Newton

A Run through Russia
the story of a visit to Count Tolstoi

ISBN/EAN: 9783337299651

Printed in Europe, USA, Canada, Australia, Japan

Cover: Foto ©Andreas Hilbeck / pixelio.de

More available books at **www.hansebooks.com**

A RUN THROUGH RUSSIA

THE STORY OF A VISIT

TO

Count Tolstoi

BY

WM. WILBERFORCE NEWTON

AUTHOR OF

" Priest and Man," " Life of Dr. Muhlenberg," " Summer Sermons,'
" Essays of To-day," etc.

HARTFORD
THE STUDENT PUBLISHING CO.
1894

PREFACE

My thanks are due for help in the compilation of Tolstoi's works and those of the Russian authors mentioned in this book to Mr. J. E. A. Smith of Pittsfield and the Rev. Preston Burr of Tacoma, Washington.

I am also greatly indebted to my young friend the Rev. Edwin Stanley Welles for the help and interest he has taken in the matter of proof-reading and in other ways assisting the much-embarrassed third member in this group known to his fellow travellers as

THE RECORDING ANGEL.

Pittsfield,
June 1st, 1894.

A RUN THROUGH RUSSIA;

—OR—

The Story of a Visit to Count Tolstoi.

CHAPTER I.

FROM DRESDEN TO ST. PETERSBURG.

A HAPPY thought in church-time is always, if it leads to practical results, a pre-eminently happy thought. The time and place and environment of feeling help to make us emphasize the thought in the days which come afterward, and in this way the good resolution born upon a Sunday becomes a fruitful child during the week which follows.

One Sunday, in the Russian church in the city of Dresden, in the winter of 1889, the thought came very forcibly into my mind that the next country to be visited when the true impulse of the tourist-fit came upon me, was the mysterious, half-awakened, half-developed empire of Russia.

The choir of men's voices in this Russian

temple were chanting in their rich and polysyl-
labic way one of the endless liturgies of the Greek
Church—and in some strange manner the words
of the CIII. Psalm seemed to resound through
these Russian cadences—"As far as the east is
from the west, so far hath he put our transgres-
sions from us."

At that very moment, while these worshippers
in the Greek Church were prostrating themselves
at rhythmic intervals and were touching the floor
with their foreheads, along with the undertone of
chant and the aroma of incense, within an easy
bowshot the familiar worship of the American
Episcopal Church was being rendered by the
faithful clergyman who cares for the spiritual
wants of the American colony, the rector of St.
John's Church, Dresden.

The chant in the Russian church, with its oft-
repeated refrain, "Gospodi pomilioui," found its
translated equivalent a few rods off in the well-
known petition of the Ancient Litany—used by
Anglican and American Church alike—"Lord
have mercy upon us ;" and in this symbolic act of
worship, the East and the West seemed to come
together—that which was oldest being represented by the Greek service, and that which was
newest in the evolution of Christianity being em-
phasized by the practical and vigorous graft of
our American religious life in the English-speak-
ing colony in the beautiful capital of the kingdom

of Saxony. Thus, in the very heart of Luther's land, a clear, bright, vivid spectacle of our American religious life stood side by side with the Russian temple, the symbol of all that is Eastern and Oriental; and thus, as the nearness of the East with the West made itself manifest in that spot where these two religious worlds seemed to come together, the happy thought took possession of the awakened mind, to visit Russia for one's self and realize personally all that Dean Stanley has so graphically described in his fascinating and instructive work, " The History of the Eastern Church."

There was also another motive which had its share in deciding the journey to Russia. A piece of literary work had just been brought to a close, and the writer of the finished volume felt that a little outing was his due reward for some months of steady labor in Dresden. But it is, after all, a personality which gives interest to a place—like the memory of Robertson at Brighton, or Arnold at Rugby, or Dean Stanley at Westminster, or Wordsworth at the Windermere lake country. And it was the personality of Count Leo Tolstoi which seemed to hang over the Russian situation of to-day, and to draw the mind toward that far-off land as the spot which had evolved his interesting character and strange career.

And in this way, as the door of the Greek Church closed and we waited for our friends to

come out of St. John's Church that Sunday, the
fixed determination took possession of the writer's
breast that he would go and see Count Tolstoi
somewhat after Stanley's story of " The Way I
Found Livingstone."

The Rev. Mr. Caskey, rector of St. John's
Church, Dresden, kindly loaned the note-book of
his journey through the Czar's dominions, little
realizing then, that the mendicant inquirer who
asked for his wisdom and experience would be
base enough to purloin the title of his diary—
which base act the writer acknowledges most
humbly, and makes the present thorough confession in the opening chapter of these articles—" A
Run Through Russia."

A happy thought plus another happy thought is
always the sequence which leads to pleasure and
profit and ultimate success. The second happy
thought in this series was to go and talk to the
Russian priest in Dresden about this proposed
journey.

But the priest was not at home, and though his
interesting young wife, who spoke English remarkably well, did her best to supply her husband's place, it was thought best to appoint a
time when we could talk the matter over in all its
bearings. Accordingly, the Greek priest, a typical Russian of the fair-haired, blonde type, came
to the hotel where our party was staying, and together we held a polyglot interview which lasted

a couple of hours, in which the German, French, Latin and Greek languages were used with an easy eclecticism which defied all conventional rules and usages.

This patchwork counterpane of conversation was very successful, however, in its practical results, for my friend, the Russian priest, was affable, helpful and agreeable, though it became quite evident that he was more anxious that we should rightly understand the character of the Greek Church than that we should see Tolstoi, who, as the shrug of the shoulder indicated, was considered a good deal of a heretic in the eyes of the orthodox people of Russia, of whom this priest was a fair representative.

Through his kindness, an interview was obtained with a certain Countess in Dresden, a sister of the Countess who is a lady-in-waiting to the Grand Duchess Constantine in the Marble Palace in St. Petersburg. This lady was most kind and sympathetic, and entered heartily into the plan of helping us to find Tolstoi. She very kindly sent letters in advance to her friends and relatives in St. Petersburg and to the Countess Alexandrine Tolstoi, who is a lady-in-waiting in the Winter Palace to the Empress.

In due time word came back from St. Petersburg to send on the American pilgrims to the shrine of Tolstoi without further delay ; that they would be well received and would be forwarded to Moscow or to Tula if Count Tolstoi should be at his home in either of these places.

The next step was to make sure that our passports were viséd properly, for Russia is most carefully guarded to-day, and ever since Mr. George Kennan's visit to Siberia, the American tourist is looked upon with the eagle eye of the Russian detective.

The Russian chargé in Dresden shook his head over the passports of two of the party; for, alas! they were "*geistlicher*," " clergymen "—and clergymen to-day are looked upon with suspicion by the all-powerful Pobedonestzeff, the celebrated procureur of the Holy Synod. But a kind letter from the Countess and a telegram to St. Petersburg set the matter straight, and a precious little bit of extra parchment riveted onto the original passport made everything right for us ; and thus, with our characters given to us in writing, we heeded the advice of St. Paul to his companion Timothy :

" The cloak that I left, bring with thee when thou comest, and the books, but *especially the parchment*."

And here we may as well introduce the party who were setting out on this " Run Through Russia " and were about to enter upon their search after Tolstoi.

Two of the party were clergymen and the other was a wise layman of the " Judicious Hooker " type of mind—and together they formed the most agreeable companions it was ever the lot of a solitary traveller to find.

It does not do in books, as it is not good manners in sermons, to mention names, or to be too personal in one's description; suffice it then to say, that one of these gentlemen, owing to his marked resemblance to the celebrated English novelist, shall be known as " Mr. Thackeray," while the other, because of his resemblance to the illustrious poet, will henceforth bear the proud title of " Lord Byron."

Mr. Thackeray and Lord Byron had warmed themselves to the work in an inverse ratio to the difficulties to be overcome and in a sort of geometrical progression from the kind patronage of the nobility at St. Petersburg. Together this trio of pilgrims went to that busy bee-hive of American tourists, Thode & Co., Bankers, Dresden, where we received our money which had been exchanged into roubles and copecks and where our obliging young friend, Mr. Hans Björn Graesse, arranged our letters of credit for us and gave us the necessary handsome brown rouble notes of the Russian Empire, bearing on them the dashing portrait of the Empress Catherine the Second.

The ride from Dresden to Berlin is uneventful, and Berlin itself is too markedly one of the five or six great cities of the world to bear other than a merely passing description.

The only circumstance of interest which happened on this visit to Berlin was the fact that, while Lord Byron and Mr. Thackeray were busy with some money-changers of Jewish extraction, the other member of the party, who was standing on the curbstone patiently waiting for his companions to return, had the pleasure of seeing face to face the celebrated Prince Bismarck as he drove along the Unter den Linden on his way to the Emperor's palace, and was more impressed than ever with the strong resemblance he bore to that well-known Berkshire manufacturer, the late Hon. Zenas Marshall Crane of Dalton, who for years before had been spoken of as the Berkshire Bismarck by his many admiring friends.

At 11:09 o'clock that night, April 2, 1889, the train came along that was to take this party to St. Petersburg ; so the three tourists took their places in the sleeping-car, which places had been telegraphed for in advance. The sleeping-cars in Europe are very luxurious, built as they are upon the European plan of providing an extra dressing-room for each two compartments. A very comfortable night was passed and the next morning found us bowling our way very smoothly and evenly across that long stretch of country known as Northeastern Germany, where once a portion of the ill-starred kingdom of Poland had been.

About 3 o'clock in the afternoon, while Mr. Thackeray was absorbed in a deep and profound study of the Russian language with its complex alphabet of thirty-eight letters, the invention of the Monk Cyrenius of the ninth century, Lord Byron exclaimed, " I wish we could see something which is distinctively Russian—I am tired with this familiar German scenery."

The words were scarcely out of the mouth of our poetical friend before the train passed over the little bridge of stone spanning the brook which divides Russia from Germany, and having left Eydt Kuhnen, the last stopping-place on the German line, we drew up at Wirballen, the first town on the Russian frontier.

At last we were in Russia, divided from the familiar land and language of Germany by a narrow little stream, and the wish of Lord Byron was gratified in an " augenblick," while Mr. Thackeray laid down his Russian primer and proceeded to stand the examination of the gray-coated military gentlemen who swarmed about the station like bees around a hive.

Here, at last, everything was distinctively Muscovitish ; it was but the transition of a few seconds, but it was not necessary to be officially informed that Germany was behind us, and that we had at last reached the confines of that vast country toward which we had been so long in coming. Here were veritable Cossacks, Tartar-eyed officers with double dangling swords at their sides, sadly impeding their daily walk, even if they did not interfere with their professional conversation ; and these military-looking men with their long, gray overcoats and flat, gray caps, together with the astrakhan helmets of the armed police with their breasts embroidered with a double row of cartridges and with cross daggers forming a St. Andrew's cross over their breasts, impressed upon the peaceful strangers the stern and sinister fact that they were in a land in which the old motto was inverted, a land where the sword was, indeed, mightier than the pen.

The effect of this sudden and unexpected transition from the familiar surroundings of the Fatherland to the strange surprise of this land of absolute monarchy was quite overwhelming. It seemed to be the work of an instant—like the shifting of scenes at the well-known Opera House at Dresden. Everything was changed as at the nod of the director on the stage. The quaint old German cottages, the green fields of the old landscape, the familiar German tongue, the uniforms of the German Imperial army, and the running gear of the railroad cars, were all a thing of the past now, and gave place, as by the magician's wand, to white snow, gray overcoats, a conundrum-like sign language, ubiquitous soldiers, and a distinct odor of sheepskin—that smell of leather which seemed to haunt the tourist and hover forever under his nostrils throughout all the land of Russia.

We were soon given to understand that the next thing to be done was to produce our passports, and not to be long about it either, since these almond-eyed Tartar gentlemen, with an embarrassment of riches in the way of pistols and swords, had everything in their own hands in case of any unwillingness to comply with their commands.

As good luck would have it, the writer was the first man to graduate from this examination in the dark room, and, on hearing something which sounded like his name as it might have been pronounced in the Coptic or Sanscrit tongues, passed through a small iron gate which opened into the kingdom of the Czar's elect, and secured once more his precious passport, while his friends, Lord Byron and Mr. Thackeray, were farther down the file.

While engaged in the work of trying to decipher some of the signs in the shops of this queer little town on the Russian border—Wirballen by name—a stranger approached, with hands in pocket and Derby hat far back upon the head, whereupon the following conversation ensued :

" Fellow-countryman, I believe."

" Yes, I am an American."

"Stranger, it does me good to see you. I want to get out of this land of secret police and queer language, where the letters are all drunk and run the wrong way, like lopsided crabs. I'd give my

bottom dollar if I was on the other side of that
brook."

"Well, why don't you cross over?"

"I can't do it, stranger. I'm travelling with
eight elephants and my passport has been sent
back to the Crimea to get viséd there."

"You mean that you are in a party of eight?"

"No, not that. I am agent for Barnum, and
have bought eight elephants for him out beyond
the Crimea. There they are; out there, eating
their heads off. It's no joke keeping eight elephants upon one's hands! Why, stranger, they
eat a barnful of hay every twenty-four hours, and
here I am anchored to this spot until my passport
comes back from the Crimea. You see I happened
to forget to have it signed out there, and here I
am with only that little brook yonder keeping me
from touching German soil, and yet I cannot
cross over, all because of that miserable passport
system. Stranger, I'd give a hundred dollars if I
only had them eight elephants across that brook
and safely on board the Hamburg steamer!
Just look at them eating!"

A view out of the station window, which, since
the name of Barnum had been mentioned, in some
strange way seemed to take on a resemblance
to the railway station at Bridgeport, Conn., on the
N. Y. & N. H. R. R. revealed the sight of the
eight elephants tossing hay over their heads in a
freakish sort of play, while the four keepers strove

in vain to keep the littered place in some sort of order.

The "stranger," having expressed his sympathy with his disconsolate fellow-countryman—inasmuch as he himself had been lately conducting a party of eight tourists through Europe—and having judiciously admonished his fellow "keeper" upon the sinfulness of appending a pack of firecracker oaths at the end of every sentence, turned from the picture of the playful elephants tossing to and fro their evening allowance of hay by the banks of the dividing river which separates the domain of the Russian Czar from that of the German Kaiser, to look for his lost friends and discovered by their happy faces, like schoolboys who had passed their examination, that Lord Byron and Mr. Thackeray had graduated from the Russian Custom House at Wirballen.

The important work of becoming accustomed to this strange Cossack environment was not a little helped by the judicious use of copper copecks thrown around to the assorted variety of military officials, who, with swords and daggers and carbines hanging at their sides and cartridges embroidered in rows of dozens across the breast, proved the truthfulness of the English schoolboy's prime article of belief, "Never scorn the humble brown"—the humble brown being an equivalent term for the copper penny.

Silence is golden always in Russia, especially

when preceded and followed by the distribution
of copecks, which, like charity, are ·found to
cover a multitude of sins !

At 4 o'clock in the afternoon of this same day
the train started for St. Petersburg.

The first impression in these Russian cars was
a decidedly American impression. The smoke
that came from the locomotive revealed the fact
that the fuel used was pine wood, and it seemed
at first as if one were travelling through the upper
portion of New Hampshire or in the Sunny South,
while the scenery was like that through the scrub-
oak section of the Michigan Central road through
Canada.

On every side was observed the distinct type of
the Tartar face in the soldiers, the peasants and
the police. So much impressed was one of the
party with the Orientalism of the scene that he
broke at once into the opening strain of the
" Mikado,"

" We are gentlemen of Japan,"

but the Cossack conductor, not understanding
English, took no notice of this apparent act of
indiscretion.

The next thing to be done was the mastering
of the Russian language. These tourists began
at this in reading and deciphering signs. Lord
Byron was in an ecstasy of joy when he found
that he had been able to spell " buffet," which

had the Greek letter "Phi" in the middle of it ; whereas Mr. Thackeray, the teacher of the language in this class, took great delight that he had mastered the word "scholchoi" ("How much does it cost ?") With regret, however, it must be confessed that this word appears to be reserved for some classical use ; as the natives along the road never seemed to reply to it, but carefully took the money that was offered to them and never made any change, whether they were offered rouble notes or a handful of copecks.

All the afternoon and evening the class in the Russian language continued their studies, every now and then missing their vowels and getting their consonants in the wrong place, but in every other respect being most excellent linguists.

The train for St. Petersburg was upon a single track and stopped every twenty-five or thirty minutes in order that the passengers might take refreshments at the wayside eating-houses, while the engine at the same time took wood and water. At all of these stations the peculiar Russian shrine, or "Icon," an image which is exposed for worship, was to be seen.

The Cossack conductor was a wily-looking character, who spoke only in Russian. However, he did his best to explain the nature of the country through which we were passing, which consisted of a long and weary stretch across the snow-covered fields. No towns or villages were in sight, and the only signs of life which were obtained were the little rude peasants' huts as they were clustered together in these small hamlets.

The following morning, while at breakfast at one of these eating-stations by the side of the railway, we were surprised at discovering a group of beggars—men, women and children—clad in sheepskins, with hides bound about their legs with thongs. These wretched creatures began a series of ritualistic bowing to us, the women actually going down on their knees to us and putting their heads to the ground. It was a novel sight, but before we got through with our journey we saw many specimens of the mendicant. He is on every hand in Russia and swarms like the locust in that land. This group of beggars performed their antics, all the time we were at breakfast, with the same feeling that actuated Felix when he sent for the Apostle Paul, of whom we read : " He hoped also that money should have been given him of Paul ; wherefore he sent for him that he might commune with him."

The miserable children were experts at this ritualistic performance, and they all seemed to express a great sense of relief when they reached the main element of their worship in the passing of the contribution-box. It was made of tin, so that every copeck sounded well in it ; for while these beggars believe in charity, they do not at

all despise the " sounding brass and tinkling cym-
bals."

That which strikes the traveller in passing
through this long stretch of country is the fact
that there seems to be no middle class. There
are no towns or villages, only hamlets, with
stables for sheep and other animals directly
among the dwellings of the people.

At 6 o'clock in the evening of the second day
from Dresden the sun set in sight, directly over
St. Petersburg. We could see the smoke arising
from the great city, which in some strange way
reminds one of Cleveland with its clouds of
smoke over Lake Erie.

The river Neva flows from the dark waters of
Lake Olga directly to St. Petersburg. The train
passed by the town of Gatchina, the Czar's country residence, and his royal train, which was in
readiness to take him the next day to St. Petersburg, was standing upon a side track.

As we neared the city of St. Petersburg, the
heavy smoke which hung over it seemed like a
huge pall, gray and leaden ; and at every turn,
wherever there was a road to the city, at the
crossing of the railroad track, the ubiquitous
Russian soldier could be seen with his flat, gray
cap and red band, and long, gray overcoat, acting as sentinel at the gates.

All the horses were harnessed to sledges ; the
three-horse sledge or " tritska " seems to be the

favorite vehicle, and the universal hoop or arch over the horses' heads is a distinctive feature of all Russian harness.

As our train went whirling into St. Petersburg the smoke from the resinous wood enveloped it in a cloud, and as we looked out of the window on the left, past the Emperor's palace at Gatchina, we saw a lonely Russian peasant driving his sledge toward the west as the sun was going down. He was going home, we were hurrying to St. Petersburg to the welcome of a great hotel ; the Czar was coming on behind us in his special royal train ;—what was the peasant driving home to ?

A QUAY ON THE NEVA—ST. PETERSBURG.

CHAPTER II.

ST. PETERSBURG.

THE unknown author of the Book of Kings in the Old Testament, had a very ingenuous method of referring all readers who are desirous of ascertaining further facts concerning the history of the heroes whom he mentions, to the companion book of Chronicles for obscure points connected with their lives. " Now the rest of the acts of King Hezekiah and all that he did, are they not written in the books of the Chronicles of the Kings of Judah ? "

In like manner, the writer of this story begs to refer all readers who are desirous of statistical information, to Murray's and Bædeker's guidebooks, and to the recent magazine articles in the *Century* and *Harper's*, as well as to the different books upon Russia, which have so recently been published in that lavish abundance which clearly indicates a popular interest in this vast and slowly developing country.*

* Wallace's " Russia ;" " The Story of Russia," by W. R. Morfill ; " Lectures on Russian Literature," by Ivan Panim ; T. Y. Crowell's publications of Tolstoi's works ; " Truth about Russia," by W. T. Stead ; " Britons and Muscovites," by Curtis Guild ; " Free Russia," by W. H. Dixon ; " England and Russia," by Madame Olga Novikoff; ",Skobeleff and the Slavonic Cause," by O. K.; "Impressions of Russia," by George Brandes.

The philosophy of the baker, who related his adventures in the well-known poem, "The Hunting of the Snark," comes home to one who, in the presence of all this lavish display of information and research, attempts to describe his impressions of Russia after the didactic method of the average guide-book.

> "'My Father and Mother were honest though poor—'
> 'Skip all that,' cried the Bellman in haste.
> 'If it once becomes dark we've no chance of a snark—
> We have hardly a minute to wait.'
> 'I skip forty years,' said the Baker in tears,
> 'And proceed without further remark
> To the day when you took me aboard of your ship
> To help you in hunting the snark.
> A dear uncle of mine, after whom I was named,
> Remarked, when I bade him farewell—'
> 'O, skip your dear uncle!' the Bellman exclaimed
> As he angrily tinkled his bell."

Mark Twain has declared in one of his stories that he was always willing to write obituary notices or deliver funeral orations about strangers, as in this way he was not embarrassed by facts— since it is the facts of friendship which impede and hinder the eloquent oration. Facts are sometimes extremely in the way. Let us try to be as little incommoded as possible by their presence, while truthfully giving our impressions in this story of a " Run Through Russia."

The first distinct impression of St. Petersburg on arriving is that it is, like Nineveh, "a very

great city," and very far away from the rest of
mankind. When one has travelled for forty-eight
hours along a narrow line of single-track railroad
without coming to towns or villages or junctions
or cross-roads, one begins to doubt whether there
be any St. Petersburg, after all, at the other end
of this long run, so far away does it seem ; and
the disturbing doubts which beset the crew of
Columbus begin to make their presence felt as the
endless stretch of perspective rails run on and on
towards the ever-receding North Pole.

On arriving at St. Petersburg one is impressed
at once with the haste and business activity of the
place. It seems the most like an American city
of any of the great cities of Europe, with its elegant palaces and open lots and small wooden and
brick tenements crowded together. Something
about it reminds one at once of Washington, and
of North Broad Street, Philadelphia, and of certain parts of New York, namely, Sixth, Seventh
and Eighth Avenues.

We drove at once in an omnibus along the
celebrated Nevskoi Prospekt, with its four lines
of carriages, racing, driving, tearing up and down
in alternate rows, like a four deep chariot-race in
the Coliseum of Ancient Rome. Droskies, sedate
carriages with liveried footmen and coachmen,
troitskas, or three-horse sledges, with the universal
hoop over the horses' necks, and long lumbering
wagons with peculiar and oriental harnessing, and

yet withal with a semi-western look of newness and familiarity, make this famous street seem very natural and very American in the sense of nervous haste which it imparts to all who enter it. In his article on palatial Petersburg, in the July number of *Harper's Magazine*, 1889, Mr. Theodore Child says :

"With a last glance at the Nevskoi Prospekt—the pride of every patriotic Russian—we will conclude our observations on palatial Petersburg. This famous street is remarkable first of all for its dimensions ; it is more than a hundred feet broad and three miles long.

" In this framework, admirably called a Prospect—for the whole street is calculated to produce its effect when looked at in perspective and not when examined in detail—the whole characteristic movement of St. Petersburg may be seen ; the tramways ; the strings of telegas, laden with goods ; the clouds of common droskies, looking like toy carriages ; the finer private droskies, drawn by splendid, long-stepping trotters, harnessed so lightly that the beauty of their form is nowhere concealed ; the troitskas with their team harnessed fanwise, three abreast ; the throngs of silent foot-passengers—mujiks, civil servants, officers in long gray overcoats ; women of the lower classes, wearing short dresses of pale green, unæsthetic blues, with gaudily embroidered kerchiefs on their heads ; ladies in Parisian toilettes ;

here and there queer old women, who seem to have
seen better days, and who now console themselves
by smoking cigarettes as they lounge in the sun ;
mujiks, who, in spite of the warmth, still remain
faithful to their sheepskin touloupes, and who
loaf along, dreamily cracking sunflower seeds, the
chewing of which is a favorite, popular distraction;
street-hawkers who sell ' kvas ' and other drinks,
cakes, sweets, fruit and flowers ; nursemaids
wearing the national costume, and coiffure—a sort
of tiara of blue or red velvet, embroidered with
big pearl beads ; priests in long flowing black
gowns and tall brimless hats, sometimes covered
with a veil ; Circassians with their long coats and
their breasts stiff with cartridges ; a patrol of
Cossacks ambling along on their small, nervous
little horses, with their hay-nets slung from the
saddles. Horsemen are rare in St. Petersburg,
for the Russians, do not appreciate riding as a v
pleasure. The great means of locomotion is that
foolish vehicle—the drosky—which is the most
universal and characteristic feature in Russian
street landscape."

Arriving at our destination, the Hotel de
Europe, we were cordially met and welcomed by
a stranger who seemed to be expecting us, and
when we asked his name our friend replied, " I
am James Pilley, gentlemen." Whereupon Mr.
Thackeray informed us that before starting from
Dresden he had written to engage rooms for us

and to secure the services of that eminent guide
on our visit to St. Petersburg.

James Pilley was the most remarkable guide
that it was ever our good fortune to meet.
Whether in professional or in private life, Pilley
was always most interesting. His method of hir-
ing a drosky was always unique. He would go
forth into the streets and call out in loud, lusty
tones to the assembled congregation of drosky
drivers, who would rush up to demand his favor.
At first, we thought it was a Nihilist uprising, but
later on we discovered that it was only his original
method of securing the best drosky in the vicinity.
We regret to state that the custom in vogue
whereby the drosky driver was to consider himself
rejected, was the familiar American method of
spitting on the rejected candidate. The hereto-
fore noisy, loud-spoken Russian " cabby," who up
to this point considered himself a candidate for
Pilley's favor, hereupon would take a back seat, if
such a thing could be possible in one who always
sits on the front seat of the drosky ; and Pilley
was henceforth in command of the drosky which
had made the cheapest fare for the trip. This
alarming performance was repeated every time we
wanted a conveyance. In whatever light we considered Pilley, he was always an enigma. You
might see him sleeping, like a seal on an iceberg,
among the " Dienstmen " or commissionaires in
the hotel lobby ; for Pilley's method of recruiting

his wasted energies was like that of the great Napoleon, who had the rare faculty of instantly dropping to sleep when off duty.

When Pilley was describing churches, palaces, shrines, cathedrals or the works of art therein to be found, there was no trifling with him on duty. He had about him the most unique faculty of making men and things go. "Stretch your necks, gentlemen," he would say when we were called upon to look at some far-off fresco in the ceiling of palace or cathedral, "Stretch your necks, gentlemen, there's nothing in Europe which comes near it ! "

In remonstrating with him on one occasion while threading our way through St. Isaac's Cathedral, where the worshippers, as thick as black-berries in September, were devoting themselves before a certain shrine, and where we were carried along in a careless Irish jaunting-car style—he simply replied, "Why gentlemen, this is all right, I am James Pilley."

The sights of St. Petersburg are many and were seen by the party under the direction of Mr. James Pilley in something like this manner :

" Fire tower, gentlemen ! 674 (or something like it) feet high ; bell rings whenever there is a fire— quite American-like, I am told ! "

" Tea in camels' skins, gentlemen—look 'ere sir —'ere in this window—not over there sir—'ere sir ;

tea brought over the plains all the way from China."

" Where do they get the camels' skins, Mr. Pilley ? " inquired Lord Byron.

" They call them camels' skins," replied Mr. Pilley, " but then, sir, we know that they are other skins besides camel skins, but they bring them over on the camels' backs, sir, all the same, all the way over from China."

" Funeral, gentlemen,—very poor person,—wish I could show you a regular rich funeral,—one horse and two mourners you perceive,—very poor funeral ! "

This remark of Mr. Pilley's was called forth by the sudden appearance of a horse with a black pall upon it, covering head and ears, like the covering of a knight's horse in days of heraldry and tournament.   A long wooden wagon, likewise covered with a pall, followed, on which was placed the coffin, in plain board, while two peasant women, in peculiar garb, walked behind.

" Here comes a wet nurse, gentlemen," observed the irrepressible Pilley, "she comes from the Foundling Hospital established by the Empress Catherine II., to stop the prevailing national crime of infanticide.   They have as many as eight new babies every day and can accommodate eight hundred babies at one time."

As we turned our gaze from the funeral to the nurse, we observed a huge peasant woman with a

peculiar arrangement of red head-gear and petti-
coat, and white puffs and flaps around the neck
and shoulders, who came walking along toward us
as if she were a metal doll who had been wound
up to walk, or a stuffed pin-cushion after the
familiar pattern seen at the average church fair.

St. Petersburg was dull without Pilley to enliven
it. In fact, life seemed dull after being cared for
and carried along by Pilley. He it was who laid
out for us our daily work. He consummated the
difficult and laborious work of rightly seeing the
sights of St. Petersburg. When remonstrated
with on one occasion, while he was showing us a
number of saints' bones which we thought we had
seen in other countries, he explained it by saying,
" Good gracious, gentlemen, there is no country in
the world as rich in holy bones as Russia ! "
And to say the least, this bone-factory method of
canonizing the anatomy of the saints was striking
and interesting.

After seeing the shrines and the icons in the
streets, the place where the late Czar was killed,
with the new chapel which is placed upon it, the
bazaars and gin-shops, the horse-cars, and the
cattle market, which in some way has a strange
resemblance to a Chicago or St. Louis drove-yard,
the School of Mines, and the various columns and
statues and palaces of the city, the great objects
of interest in St. Petersburg are found to be the
Winter Palace and the Hermitage, the Nevski

Monastery and Convent of St. John Nevski, the
Fortress and the Church of St. Peter and St. Paul,
and the Cathedrals of St. Isaac and of Our Lady
of Kazan, and the hut and boat of Peter the Great,
in both of which he lived, while he, like immortal
cyclops, worked at the creation of St. Petersburg.

The cathedrals and the monastery we will consider in a later chapter ; the Winter Palace and
the Hermitage deserve a chapter in this story for
themselves alone. Let us, in the remainder of
this chapter, go round about this wonderful city
of his taste—this creation of the will and the
genius of Russia's most potent personality—Peter
the Great—palatial Petersburg.

There is no such striking personality in the
history of any country of Europe as that of the
illustrious Peter the Great. In St. Petersburg at
every turn, in the famous Hermitage Gallery, in
the celebrated fortress of Peter and Paul (the
Westminster Abbey of Russia), by picture, statue
and public work at every turn his memory is pre-
served and honored as the great founder of this
young empire. To the American visitor there is
much about Peter the Great which reminds one of
our own Benjamin Franklin. He strikes us as a
Franklin who, by some wave of fate, happened to
be born the heir to a throne. He has the same
broad forehead, indicative of the faculty of mechanical invention. How this man could have
accomplished so much in fifty years is an everlast-

ing cause of wonder. His work-room, his lathes and machines, the boat he built, the travelling carriage he invented—strangely like our modern American buck-board—his tools, trunks, bookcases, hampers, furniture and inventions of all kinds remind the American visitor very markedly of the handicraft tendency of Benjamin Franklin, who lightened the hours of his anxious days of statesmanship with the muscular delights of physical exercise.

In "The Story of Russia," by W. R. Morfill, the latest volume in "The Story of the Nations" series, his work and character are thus described : " It is difficult to estimate accurately the Titanic figure of Peter. He was a strange mixture of virtues and vices. Inheriting all the traditions of despotism, we must not feel surprised if, like our own Edward I. he had no scruple in removing any obstacles which appeared in his path. To the same source must be traced his lack of self-rule and physical restraint. He was descended, we must remember, from a long line of semi-Asiatic barbarians, and if he had not been a man of powerful genius, would have been content, as they were, with the idleness and luxury of a palace—

' Like one of nature's fools who feed on praise.'

He was willing to abandon all these pleasures, so captivating to the ordinary mind, to put himself, as it were, to school, to endure privations and

labor, in order to break with a system against
which his intellect rebelled. There was genius
in his sense of the dignity of labor and his un-
quenchable thirst for knowledge. The active
brain was ever at work ; all persons who came in
contact with him were struck with the vigor and
originality of his mind—and not the least, William
III., one of the wisest sovereigns of his day. The
reverse of the medal is less pleasing—his reckless-
ness of human life, his intemperance, and the
brutality shown to his miserable son. Had he
been a Turkish Sultan this last-mentioned crime
would have been according to the natural order
of things ; but the strong European side of Peter
makes us forget his Asiatic training.

"Many have challenged the utility of the inno-
vations which he introduced into Russia. Would
it not have been better, they say, to have allowed
the country to develop itself gradually and not to
force upon it a premature ripeness ? But to this
it may be answered that all the best men who
had written on Russia, under the old order of
things saw that amelioration could only result
from without. Such was the opinion of Krizhan-
ich and Kotishikhin—two shrewd observers of the
seventeenth century. At the beginning of his
reign Peter found Russia Asiatic, he left her
European. He created a navy and gave her an
outlet on the Baltic, the attempt to force a passage by the embouchure of the Don at Azov hav-

ing failed. Instead of the disorderly, badly-ac-
coutered regiments of the Streltsi, he gave to
Russia an army clothed and disciplined on the
European model. He added many provinces to
the empire, constructed canals, developed many
industries, and caused serviceable books to be
translated into Russian, so that his ignorant subjects might be instructed. He gave Russia libra-
ries and museums, galleries of painting and of
sculpture ; and, finally, from an obscure barbaric
power, isolated from her European sister kingdoms, he created a powerful empire, recognized
as one of the most important states and able to
make its voice heard in the councils of Europe.
Many volumes of anecdotes about this remarkable man have been published. They show him
abounding in lively sallies, quick-witted and
shrewd, simple in his tastes and with the natural
contempt of a man of genius for pomp and milli-
nery. No man enjoyed more—perhaps even in a
boyish manner—scandalizing the proprieties of
conventional persons, immersed in ignorance and
conceit, such as those with whom Russia
abounded. For the pompous boyars to see their
Tsar sometimes going about without an attendant
and wearing an old shabby blue coat—or showing
them a pair of horse-shoes which he had made—
or sitting smoking a pipe with a newly-arrived
Dutch or English skipper, must indeed have been
an indescribable shock. He honors now and then

heretics like Gordon and Lefort, by accepting an
invitation to dine at their houses, and standing
godfather to their children. But again we think
of the reverse of the medal, the paroxysms of rage
and the ruthlessly cruel punishments. The man
is from beginning to end an enigma ; but it is impossible to deny his claims to genius, or to the
title which has been ungrudgingly assigned him
—Peter the Great."

The foundation-stone of the Cathedral of St.
Peter and St. Paul was laid by Peter the Great,
on the 16th of May, 1703, and the edifice was consecrated in the year 1733. Every one knows the
story of its triple strokes by lightning and of the
adventurous exploit of the Russian peasant who,
in the year 1803, with simply a rope and a nail,
climbed up the tall, thin tapering spire, 158 feet
high, to replace the damaged globe and cross.
" All the sovereigns of Russia," says Murray, lie
buried in the Cathedral, excepting only Peter II.,
who died and was interred at Moscow. The
bodies are deposited under the floor of the Cathedral, the marble tombs above only marking the
sites of the grave. The tomb of Peter the Great
should be visited first. It lies near the south door,
opposite the image of St. Peter. The image, with
its rich gold frame, gives Peter's stature at his
birth, viz. : 19¼ inches, as well as his breadth 5¼
inches. His consort, Catherine I., lies buried in
the same vault. The tomb of Catherine II., is the

THE CATHEDRAL OF ST. PETER AND ST. PAUL IN THE FORTRESS.—ST. PETERSBURG.

third to the right of the altar-screen. The row of tombs on the north side of the Cathedral begins with that of the Emperor Paul. The image of St. Paul opposite to it gives the height and breadth of that sovereign at birth.

The diamond wedding-ring of the Emperor Alexander is attached to the image near his tomb. The sarcophagus of the Grand Duke Constantine, brother of Nicholas I., will be recognized by the keys of the fortress of Modlin and Zamoscz, in Poland, which lie on it. The Emperor Nicholas lies in the aisle opposite the tomb of Peter the Great, while the grave of his grandson and namesake—the deeply lamented Tsesarevitch, who died at Nice in 1865—will easily be recognized in the same aisle by the palm-branches and garland of roses deposited upon it by those who so deeply mourn his loss.

The walls are almost concealed by military trophies, standards, flags, keys of fortresses, shields and battle-axes taken from the Swedes, Turks, Persians, Poles and French. The devices on the flags will be a sufficient indication of their origin.

The fortress is used as a state prison. Alexis, the eldest son of Peter the Great, having been persuaded to return from Germany, was arraigned for treason and imprisoned in the dreary casemates of this dungeon, where his father visited him immediately previous to his sudden death.

The conspirators of 1825 were confined and tried, and some executed within its walls. The cells are not shown to visitors, but the Cathedral is open all day. The Imperial Mint stands within the walls and may be viewed by visitors on application.

There is no more impressive sight in all Russia than the tombs of the Czars and Grand Dukes in this famous fortress church, with the keys of the towers and fortresses which they have conquered reposing, with the dust of ages upon them, on the broad surface of the sarcophagus or monument.

"The keys of Death and Hell," held by the Master of life, seemed fittingly symbolized by these heavy, dusty fortress keys—only the conqueror, Death, being in turn conquered by Him who had destroyed death.

On one of the marshy islands, upon which Peter the Great built his "*window looking out toward Europe*," is situated his cottage—this being the first house built by Peter on the banks of the Neva, in the year 1703. It is not very far from the fortress and is situated on the same island. There are two rooms and a kitchen in this ·wooden cottage and what was formerly Peter's bedroom is now used as a chapel.

The famous image of the Saviour, endowed with miraculous properties, which was always the companion of Peter the Great in his battles and succored his hard-pushed forces so remarkably (as he believed) at the battle of Poltáva, is suspended to the wall and is the object of the most profound adoration on the part of faithful devotees.

Peter's famous boat, the remains of its canvas and the rude workman's bench on which he sat at his door—like old Caspar at Blenheim, when his long day's work was done—are all shown to the curious visitor with an interest on the part of the custodian which shows how strong and living is the effect of Peter the Great's personality to-day.

In fact, the most wonderful object seen in all Russia was this famous boat. Whether he obtained those wonderful lines of bow and stern from the Dutch boat-builders at Zaandam or the English mechanics at the dockyards of Deptford, it is difficult to find out.

The long sharp cutter-like lines of this famous boat, made by Peter's own hands, are a lasting monument to his wonderful prevision of the age which was to come afterward; so that, while with one hand this famous Czar touched the old Muscovite world and life of Asia, with the other hand he touched the marvellous developments of the present age in which our lot is cast.

It was this wonderful dockyard experience of his at the little Dutch town of Zaandam which, after all, immortalizes this barbaric Czar and gives him a place in the hearts of all young and enthusiastic readers of history, as they remember

that pathetic German song in Lortzing's Opera
of " Czar and Zimmerman."

" Selig, O selig, ein Kind noch zu sein ! "

I.

In childhood I dallied with sceptre and crown,
And warred with my playmates, who shrank at my frown :
The sword from its scabbard how proudly I drew,
Then back to the arms of my father I flew,
And as he caressed me—" My boy," thus quoth he,
" How happy, how happy a child still to be ;
How happy, how happy a child still to be ! "

II.

In manhood I'm wearing that crown on my brow,
The weal of my Russians stamps care on it now ;
In peace or in war for their glory I strive,
Though little they love me, who cause them to thrive.
In purple robes shrouded, all's lonely for me—
How happy, how happy a child still to be !

III.

When ended each struggle, the Czar's life has flown,
His subjects will raise him a tablet of stone ;
But scarce in their hearts will his name live a day,
For all earthly greatness is doomed to decay ;
Yet Thou sayest, Almighty, " In peace come to Me "—
And happy in heaven Thy child shall I be !

But still to the minds of these tourists in St.
Petersburg, like the burden of the prophets of
old, there hung over us the burden of our mission
to Russia. As the burden of Nineveh pressed

heavily upon the soul of the wayward Jonah, so the burden of Tolstoi pressed down our keen and inquisitive spirits.

We who had started forth to find out the great prophet of the Slavic race, ought not to be trifling away our time amid the art beauties of the Hermitage or the historic sights of St. Petersburg. So it came to pass that on a Friday evening Mr. Thackeray and the writer found their way to the Marble Palace, with their letters of introduction from their friend the Russian Countess in Dresden.

A great elegance, in gorgeous red and yellow small clothes and draperies, who was found afterwards designated in our note-book as "The Tiger Lily"—with black cockade hat and silver mace, ushered us into the interior of the palace courtyard, between a couple of grenadiers armed with muskets and bayonets, while another elegance led the way into the presence of the Countess, who was lady-in-waiting to the Grand Duchess Constantine.

In the presence of these Russian grenadiers Mr. Thackeray looked as if his last hour had come, and had the air generally of a Nihilist spy about to be led to immediate execution. But a delightful cup of tea from the smoking samovar in the boudoir of the Countess soon revived him ; while the very bright and sparkling conversation of the gifted Madame Novikoff, the friend of the

Countess, soon made the guests feel very much at home.

Madame Novikoff is the sister of Lieutenant-General Alexander Kireff (of whom mention will be made later on), and resides a part of the year in London, where she has written a number of striking works on Russia and the Russian situation.

She has written the books entitled " England and Russia," " Skobeleff and the Slavonic Cause," and a number of war articles on the Russian campaigns in the *Nineteenth Century* magazine. Her *nom-de-plume* in these recent articles is " O. K." for Olga Kireff, her maiden name ; and when the Countess assured us that Madame Novikoff was " O. K." we smiled blandly while inwardly wondering how a bit of American schoolboy slang ever came to find a domicile for itself in the palace of a Russian Grand Duke.

Our friend the Countess K——, assured us that the Countess Tolstoi was waiting for us to present ourselves at the Winter Palace, and reminded us that while we might at a safe distance be enthusiastic over Count Leo Tolstoi, there was a nearer view which was not all glitter, since after the manner of a one-sided fanatic, he had dared to set himself against society, government, and the Holy Orthodox Eastern Church.

Upon inquiring when we could best see the Countess Tolstoi, our hostess remarked to

MADAME OLGA NEVIKOFF,
(*the Russian War Correspondent "O. K."*)

Madame Novikoff, "Let me see; the Emperor came up from Gatchina the day before yesterday —well, there will be lunch at one o'clock to-morrow—but by three you will find the Countess disengaged."

This sounded just as if it was Cousin John who had come up from Cape Cod to Boston, while it occurred to us that we, too, came up from Gatchina that same day. But as our thought remained unexpressed we failed to receive an invitation to meet the Czar—a calamity he has never dreamed of to this day.

Pilley, at the door, covered us up in his usual nurserymaid manner with a couple of shawls, and gave us quite another view of the literature on Russia and the distinguished authoress of whom mention has been made. But, as Mr. Pilley has a lucrative position at present, and is useful to strangers in Russia, we refrain from quoting his brief but impressive remark.

On the following day we paid our respects to the Countess Tolstoi at the Winter Palace. This lady was most kind and gracious in her reception, and gave us letters to the Tolstoi family in Moscow which were most helpful. Indeed all the letters given during our visit to Russia were a great help to us in preparing the way, step by step, for the far-off object of our search.

The servant in livery ushered us into a cozy parlor, where a fire was burning on the hearth, and where we discovered the Countess Tolstoi at work with a lady friend, embroidering an immense sampler which was rolled over a long cylinder, so that it resembled very much a huge musical box or orchestra cylinder, or a reel of woolen ' fabric just from the loom.

The ubiquitous samovar upon the table furnished us our indispensable cup of tea, without which, in Russia, it would seem that no conversation can be attempted.

Another elegance in blue daisies and white stockings, similar to the gentleman already described at the Marble Palace, served us at lunch, so that, altogether, it seemed very much like a parish call or a lunch preparatory to a parish guild or parochial fair.

The Countess Tolstoi, like her companions in the other palace, uttered a warning, Cassandra-like cry of regret over the distinguished object of our journey to Moscow. "Ah!" she said, "if Leo would only let his reforms alone and keep to his novels, how much better it would be for us all."

This, of course, was her sentiment before the publication of " The Kreutzer Sonata "—what her views upon the subject may be now we cannot, of course, know.

As we met the faithful, but unsearchable and inscrutable Pilley at the door, he remarked, "Stretch your necks, gentlemen,—look up the

THE WINTER PALACE—ST. PETERSBURG.

staircase! That is the Grand Duke Vladimir, brother of the Czar, he is going to a state dinner at the Winter Palace—the Czar is upstairs on the second landing."

But even this hint to the Grand Duke Vladimir failed to secure for us an invitation to the imperial dinner party—and so we returned to the Hotel de Europe, to the lonely and envious Lord Byron, who had been playing the part of Cinderella, left by her more fortunate sister, who had gone to the ball.

We told him of our American republican simplicity, like that of Franklin at the court of Versailles, and how we had enjoyed ourselves at the lunch so kindly given, but we refrained from communicating the fact that Mr. Pilley's hint made no effect upon the mind of Vladimir, as he ascended the staircase of the famous Winter Palace.

CHAPTER III.

THE two great sights of St. Petersburg are the Winter Palace and the Hermitage. There are churches and statues and columns and palaces and shrines and monasteries at every turn ; but the Winter Palace and the Hermitage are, after all, the two most important objects of interest in the great capital of Russia.

We were dragooned through these two buildings under the marching orders of Mr. James Pilley ; the two cardinal doctrines which have been preached by Tolstoi, of passive obedience and non-resistance, being the foundation truths of all peaceful relationship with our omniscient guide and all-powerful dictator.

And now while Pilley is securing the droskies in which to carry these visitors to the palace and the museum, let a word or two of description be given, and let it be in the words of one whose graphic pen has made Palatial Petersburg familiar to our American magazine readers.

" The initiative of the Russians in art and in civilization is limited. Hitherto they have displayed greater aptitude for copying than for original conception, and even for their copies they have had recourse to Western artists, particularly to Italian architects like Quarenghi, Rossi, and Count Rastrelli. The last is responsible both for the outside and the inside of the Winter Palace. This enormous structure was begun in 1732, finished in 1762, partly burned in 1837, but rebuilt in 1839 from the original drawings. It is a broad rectangular block, four stories, or about eighty feet high, with a frontage 455 feet in length and a breadth of 350 feet, one façade parallel with the Neva, another looking toward the Admiralty, the third facing the vast Alexander Place, and the fourth (blind) façade backing up to the adjoining Hermitage Palace, with which it communicates by means of a covered bridge.

"The proportions of this palace are not commendable ; the style of architecture is very bombastic rococo ; the decoration is overcharged with statues, caryatides, flower-pots, grenades, and trumpery accessories. The cheap stucco surface of its façades—mercilessly broken up by pilasters, water-spouts, and windows, so that the eye nowhere finds repose—is washed with a brownish red, terra-cotta color, picked out with a lighter tone of yellow. The iron roof is painted red.

"The outside of this palace is absolutely without charm or merit of any kind, its only claim to notice is its immensity, which, by the way, according to Russian notions, is a very considerable claim.

" The interior is a saddening example of the bad taste which seems to characterize crowned heads of all nations, whether the Russian Czar, the Turkish Sultan, the German Emperor, or the British sovereign. The ornamentation is for the most part in rampageous rocaille style, bright burnished gold on whitewash, or imitation white marble.

"Our pen absolutely refuses to describe the sham splendor of the imperial apartments, with their modern French polished furniture and vile wood-carving, their massive screens glazed with purple glass, their wall-hangings of yellow and white, or rose and green satin. The malachite room, the Pompeiian room, the Mauresque bath-room, likewise failed to transport us with admiration.

" The corner that pleased us best was Peter the Great's throne-room, whose walls were hung with soft, red velvet, embroidered with golden eagles. The St. George's Hall, a parallelogram, 140 feet by 60 feet, adorned with Corinthian columns of real white marble, with gilt bases and capitals, is also a fine room, perhaps the finest in the whole palace. The White Hall, the Golden Hall, and the Nicholas Hall are chillingly white show-rooms, which require the animation of the court ceremonies and balls and the glitter of lights and diamonds, in order to give them a picturesque interest.

" Finally we may notice the state entrance to

the palace from the Neva Quay, called the Ambassadors' Stairs, of white Carrara marble, and the vestibule, richly decorated and gilded with Renaissance ornaments and statuary. This staircase and the St. George's Hall are the only two parts of the Winter Palace that present an aspect of real grandeur and majesty.

"The adjoining Palace of the Hermitage, likewise of stucco, colored in two shades of café-au-lait, was built between 1840 and 1850 by a Munich architect, Leopold von Klenze, in a sort of Greek style.

"It forms an immense parallelogram, 512 feet by 375 feet, with two large courts. One main façade fronts along the street called the Million-naja, where is the entrance, under an imposing vestibule, supported by ten colossal Atlas figures, twenty-two feet high, carved out of dark gray granite. In niches along this façade, which is colored to imitate stone, are statues of eminent artists, cast in zinc, to imitate bronze.

"Entering the palace, we find ourselves in a noble hall, the roof of which is supported by sixteen monolithic columns of Finland granite, terminating in capitals of Carrara marble. The stairs, in three flights, are of real marble, but the walls on either side are of yellow imitation marble.

"The rooms of the Hermitage in which the pictures and other collections are lodged, are for the most part sumptuously decorated and adorned with gigantic candelabra, vases and tables of malachite, porphyry, or jasper, and many splendid pieces of French furniture of the eighteenth century."*

In the matter of art treasures, some of the most interesting and attractive objects in the Winter Palace were as follows : the emperor's great jubilee room ; the dining-room where the famous bomb explosion took place ; the malachite drawing-room ; the cabinet of the Emperor Nicholas I., like that of Sir Walter Scott at Abbotsford ; the stairway up to the Nicholas Hall, of which Mr. Pilley remarked " Look at it, gentlemen, look at it ! the greatest stairway in Europe— nothing on earth to touch it, gentlemen !"

Then follows the St. George's Hall, the famous Throne Room and the Memorabilia of Russia's two illustrious Czars—Peter the Great and Nicholas I.

The iron death-bed of Nicholas I., when he returned from the Crimea a broken-hearted man, is a striking souvenir, resembling, as it does, the small iron bedstead on which Napoleon I. died at St. Helena. The room where the late Emperor died after the explosion ; the dying bed-chamber of the Empress ; the broken bits of furniture in the doomed dining-room and the shattered carriage of Alexander II. are striking and suggestive objects of interest, showing as they do the thorny

* " Palatial Petersburg," by Theodore Child, *Harper's Magazine*, July, 1889.

path of the crowned and kingly Russian autocrats. The impression left upon the tired brain, after a day spent among the art treasures of the Hermitage, is that of the wild phantasmagoria of an ever-changing kaleidoscope.

We have had a glimpse of Russian art in the wonderful collection of the painter Vasseli Verestchagin, and the teaching by his brush in the pictures of the "Siege of Plevna," "After the Battle," "Jesus on the Lake of Gennesaret," and "The Execution of the Nihilists," is as powerful in its way as Tolstoi's preaching is by pen.*

* Since writing the above, the following letter from Count Tolstoi's daughter has been received, which shows the religious development of the latest Russian art.

YASNAYA POLIANA, June 11, 1890.

DEAR MR. NEWTON : My father thanks you very much for sending yours and your brother's excellent books, which he has read with great pleasure. He now begs a favor of you, which he hopes you will grant him. At the picture exhibition of this year in St. Petersburg, there has been exposed a work of one of our renowned professors of painting, Mr. Gay, a friend of my father's and also a fellow-believer of his. One of his—Mr. Gay's—early pictures, "The Last Supper," produced a great sensation, not only in Russia, but also in Europe. The subject of this new picture is "Christ Before Pilate," or "What is Truth?" The picture excited quite contradictory feelings of applause and denigration, and was taken off the exhibition by the authorities. The chief value of the picture consists in its quite new realistic and deeply religious understanding of Christ's personality. This picture is now being taken to America. My father thinks that the American public is more able than any other to judge and appreciate the merit of it. My father hopes that you will not refuse to explain to the public the meaning and the importance of the picture. He thinks that by its deep religious truth, this picture of Mr. Gay's can serve the aim which you pursue, of uniting in one all the different Christian confessions.

Believe me, sir, yours truly,

TATIANA TOLSTOI.

But the Hermitage is an ever increasing wonder as one goes deeper and deeper in. Arvazof-
sky's painting of "Sunset on the Black Sea" is a
picture which can never be effaced from the
mind. His painting of "The Deluge" is wild
and awful, but not so impressive as the former
picture. "The Creation of the World" is
another of his remarkable efforts. "The
Nymphs in Water," by Neff, is remarkable for its
flesh-tints. "The Brazen Serpent," by Bruni,
and "The Last Day of Pompeii" are also striking and important specimens of the Russian
School.

But Mr. James Pilley preferred the classical
pictures of the old masters to these new Russian
paintings, and so we were hurried along "stretching our necks" and "looking at this" and "looking at that," with the oft-repeated reminder
snapping in our ears like the crack of the whip in
the ears of a blinded and obstinate mule, "Nothing in Europe to touch it—nothing, gentlemen!
Look at it! LOOK AT IT!" This second command being always given with tremendous and
Czar-like emphasis.

"Twenty-four Murillos, gentlemen—think of it
—twenty-four in one collection!"

"Statue of Nicholas I.—handsomest man in all
Europe. Nothing to touch him, gentlemen! A
Van Dyck—look at it. Hangels and Hinglish
partridges—hangels in the foreground, partridges

on the fly. 'Dead Boy and Dolphin,' by Ralph-fyal—only sculpture he ever made. Look 'ere sir, close by this 'ot hair flue, 'ere you have six Rembrandts! Look at this one, sir—Flemish hangels a-flopping;" this being the interpretation of a picture by Rembrandt of some angels, with distinctly Flemish faces, engaged at prayer.

But enough. Here were Steens, and Snyders, and Guido Reni's, and Teniers, and Paul Potter, and Quentin Matsys, and Titian, and Domenichino, and Wouverman, with his delightful and executive war pictures, in every one of which was found the irrepressible white horse on a gallop, and Leonardo da Vinci, and Raphael, and Fra Angelico, and Correggio, and Luti's famous "Flageolet Boy," and Michael Angelo's "Tour de Force."

Lord Byron wanted to be put to bed on arriving at the hotel, while Mr. Thackeray vainly strove to write out in his diary his impressions of the Winter Palace and the Hermitage.

"One more such victory and we are undone!" remarked Lord Byron.

"I hope you are satisfied," inquired James Pilley.

"Oh, more than satisfied!" replied all three in a breath, "but no more sight-seeing for twenty-four hours, Mr. Pilley."

Hereupon Pilley descended in the elevator and was found among the dientsmen in the hotel

lobby, sleeping sideways on his chair like a fat
sleek seal on a cool and congenial iceberg.

NOTE TO CHAPTER III.

It was the intention of the writer to include in the present
chapter a brief account of Russian Art and Artists, as sug-
gested by the pictures in the Hermitage collection of the
Russian artists there.   But there is no such definite and
technical thing as Russian Art, and the history of Russian
Art is only, after all, the history of the individual artists who
have from time to time appeared upon the stage of history.

Vasseli Verestchagin's pictures, as exhibited in our American cities, with his descriptions and his essays on realism,
have made the public familiar with this great apostle of
realistic art, and any further description of these now familiar
works of art is therefore omitted from this story of a " Run
Through Russia."

CHAPTER IV.

THE interesting events of Saturday evening at the Winter Palace were forgotten by the travellers upon the next day, which proved to be a bright and auspicious Sunday, bringing with it, even in the crowded streets of St. Petersburg, that distinctly Sunday feeling which always hems in the life of those who have kept Sunday in the past. There is a distinctly Saturday feeling and a distinctly Sunday feeling and a distinctly Monday feeling, go where we will and stay where we may. It is the influence of the past life making itself felt in the life of the present, whatever the present may be.

On this beautiful Sunday in St. Petersburg, church after church was visited. Along the Nevskoi Prospekt, and under the somewhat subdued guidance of the ever adequate Pilley, a famous monastery was visited, with its chapels and attending houses making quite a village in itself ; while through the corridors of this building and along the walks of its consecrated gardens, groups of monks of all ages could be seen. Sunday also brought us to the celebrated convent of

the Cistercians, situated upon a street where
the famous Russian abattoir is built, which,
with its bison's horns as a sign over the entrance,
strangely reminded us of a similar place in
the city of Chicago. Back to the Cathedral of
St. Peter and St. Paul, along the Nevskoi Prospekt, near the Admiralty spire and gardens, into
the Smolni Cathedral, to the chapel building upon ·
the spot where the late Emperor received his
death-wound, into the magnificent spaciousness
of St. Isaac's Cathedral, and into the grand interior of Our Lady of Kazan, these travellers
threaded their way like the detectives of Wilkie
Collins' story, who mingled with the busy throngs
in the great cities of Europe, that they might
bring back again to their temple the precious
moonstone which had been stolen and the fetich
they were set to guard. St. Isaac's Church is the
grandest temple in St. Petersburg. It was begun
about the year 1820 and finished in 1860. Great
simplicity marks this cathedral, which is built
upon the model of a Greek cross. The cathedral
of Our Lady of Kazan in the Nevskoi Prospekt is
the second cathedral in St. Petersburg. Leading
up to it on either side is a colonnade formed of
136 Corinthian columns, said to have been built
after the model of the famous colonnade at St.
Peter's at Rome. The famous 56 monoliths in
the interior of this cathedral, of Finland granite,
36 feet high, together with the flags wrested from

the Turks in many battle-fields, and the keys of
Polish fortresses, make the interior peculiarly interesting. Over every Russian place of worship,
and crowning the subdued murmur of the prayers
of the worshippers, there rise at rhythmic intervals the rich and mellifluous voices of the male
singers, who are unaccompanied by organ or any
instrument of music. Strangely effective are the
minor cadences of these mixed choirs of men and
boys, inclining every now and then to the low
wail of Eastern and barbaric people. Like a rich
resonont echo again and again from the sanctuary
at St. Isaac's and at Our Lady of Kazan, that day
we heard coming to us, borne over that flood of
many voices the old but by this time familiar
refrain—" Gospidi Pomilon, Gospidi Pomilon "—
" Lord have mercy upon us." * The prostrations
on the floor, the incessant genuflections, the kiss-
ing of the icons and the lifting-up of little children all over the church to kiss these sacred
pictures and to see the priests in the distance,
the handing of lighted tapers from those in the
rear of the assemblage to their friends who were
nearer the great candelabra, the rich voices of the
priests who seemed by the sequence of their tones
to be going through a never-ending liturgy,—

* " As Eastern Christians will recite the ' Kyrie Eleison,' the ' Gospidi Pomilon' in a hundred-fold repetition . . . so the four hundred
and fifty prophets of Baal performed their wild dances round their
altar.' —DEAN STANLEY, " *History of the Jewish Church*," second series, page 333.

are elements which make the Russian place of
worship something that can never be forgotten
through all after-time.

When the morning's work was over, the writer
and Mr. Thackeray entered the one Roman Catholic church in St. Petersburg, situated not far
from the Hotel de Europe upon the Nevskoi
Prospekt. It is strange to think of the Roman
Catholic as being a dissenter in Russia, where
this Church holds its place among the other
churches only on suffrance, so long as its preaching is in no wise aggressive towards the Holy
Orthodox Eastern Church. When we entered
this Roman Catholic church we found a tonsured
friar preaching from the mediæval pulpit with a
warmth and fire which seemed truly Western and
familiar. The foolishness of preaching never
seemed such wisdom as it did upon that memorable Sunday at St. Petersburg, when throughout
the entire length and breadth of the Russian
churches in that great metropolis not a sound or
word of preaching was heard. Mr. Thackeray
and his companion glowed inwardly upon hearing
the voice of a preacher again, and felt with
Simon Peter on the Mount of Transfiguration,
that it was indeed good for them to be there.

It is very evident to any who look deeply into
this subject, that the upper classes in Russia have
a conventional faith in the Christian religion, and
look upon the Church and clergy as an arm of

power, side by side with the army and the secret
police, which must in any wise be maintained.
Nothing stronger with reference to the religious
life of Russia has ever been written than Mr. W.
T. Stead's book entitled "Truth about Russia."
For any who would like to pursue this line
of thought, his fourth chapter, entitled "The
Tribune of all the Russias," is commended as
containing a fund of information upon this subject. In one place in this interesting book he
says :

"'The first dogma of the Christian religion,'
said Count Tolstoi to me as we walked along the
chaussée that leads from Toula to Kieff, 'is the
doctrine of the Trinity. For nine hundred years
our Church has had the peasantry absolutely in
her own hands ; and how many of the peasants
do you think have any notion of what the Trinity
is ?' I did not venture to guess. The Eastern
Church lays great stress upon the dogma of the
Trinity—a difference of opinion as to the precise
origin of the third person of the Trinity being an
insurmountable obstacle in the way of the re-
union of Christendom. If the Church had been a
living, teaching force, instead of being a more or
less automatic performer of ceremonies, the doctrine of the Trinity would have been mastered by
every peasant ; for it is the special boast of the
dominant school that there are no *confessionslose*
people in Russia. Every Orthodox must take the

Communion at least once a year. No one can get married without going to Confession and to Mass. Judge, then, my surprise when Count Tolstoi continued, ' Not one peasant in ten—I sometimes think, not one in a hundred—has the least idea of what the Church's doctrine of the Trinity is. I have asked them over and over again, and they usually give very extraordinary answers. I must have questioned some hundreds of pilgrims as to their idea of the doctrine of the Trinity, and of these hundreds I do not remember six who could even name the persons of the Trinity. As a rule, they say that the Trinity consists of Jesus, the Virgin, and St. Nicholas. But we will ask the next pilgrim whom we meet, and you shall hear for yourself.'

" We had not long to wait. Seated on a little knoll by the side of the road there were three or four pilgrims. Two of them seemed mere tramps, but a mother and son were much above the average, and to her Count Tolstoi addressed himself. She said she was on the road to Kieff ; her son had fallen into the river, and had been rescued from drowning. In gratitude to God she had vowed to make a pilgrimage to Kieff with her boy, and she was on her way thither. She was therefore a good pilgrim, not a mere tramp, but one who was fulfilling a religious duty. But when asked about the Trinity she replied, ' Oh yes, I know all about the Trinity ; there were three

brothers who were thrust into a cave and set on
fire, and in the fire Jesus came and walked with
them. I have read all about it in the Gospel;'
and she was going off into fresh detail when the
Count stopped her. 'There,' said he, 'you have
a fair sample; she thinks the three Hebrew
children were the Trinity. That is the net result
of nine hundred years of dogmatic teaching by a
Church which has had exclusive possession of the
field.' . . .

" The best thing that could happen to Russia—
better even than the sudden determination of the
Emperor to shake off the trammels of his *entour-
age*, and to appear among his subjects as a hard-
riding Tzar, determined to see with his own eyes,
and hear with his own ears, all that is going on
in his dominions—would be a great spiritual revival within the Eastern Church. Here and
there the earnest voice of an eloquent priest is
heard, amidst the monotonous chant of the un-
ending liturgies, pleading for a religious life that
will be other than merely formal; but for the
most part these voices find no echo, and sometimes, if the accent is at all strange, the preacher
is silenced altogether. The Church, with its
ecclesiastics, does not, as a rule, concern itself
about the mundane affairs of this life. The
Service of Man (save as an immortal spirit whose
blessedness hereafter can best be secured by the
recitation of a certain number of creeds, and the

performance of ceremonies) is a matter which it
regards too often as beneath its notice. I do not
say—it would be a monstrous and wicked exag-
geration to say—that a great spiritual apparatus,
designed to furnish these millions with the Water
of Life, has gone utterly to rust and ruin. It has
reared, and still rears, saints holy and noble as
are to be found in any Church; but regarded
solely from a mundane point of view, and looked
at with the eye of a purely secular person, who
can only judge of religious systems by the extent
to which they minister to the wants, stimulate
the consciences and satisfy the intellectual needs
of men, the Russian Church stands sorely in need
of whatever impetus can be given to it from without. I do not suppose that any foreign church
can ever make much headway in Russia; the
national spirit is too strong; the instinct and traditions of centuries are too deeply rooted.
Neither can anyone wish to see the Eastern
Church torn by divisions such as those which
have rent the Western Church in twain. But
until Russia has a priest in every village who is
intelligent, pious, and sober, and a Church which
recognizes that its duty is to minister to the
daily wants and daily needs of humanity, and not
merely to say Masses for our souls hereafter—is
it not suicidal folly to close the door to the widest
possible influx of other forms of Christian faith?
Instead of vetoing propaganda, even of mistaken

creeds, would it not be better to welcome it as the most efficacious way by which the Orthodox can be roused to make a counter-propaganda? Better schism than sleep; better divisions than death. And the best and the simplest remedy against somnolence and paralysis in religion, as in business, is free and open competition."

Further on in this book, in speaking about the tyranny of Pobedonestzeff, the procurator of the Russian synod, he says:

"Against the Catholic Poles, against the German Lutherans, M. Pobedonestzeff may wage war with some plausible semblance of justification. But against the Stundists, against the Molokani, against the Pashkoffski, against the Evangelicals of every shade, only the incorrigible perversity of the persecutor can find a pretext for prosecuting a campaign of extermination. This is a matter far more serious for the Power that persecutes than it is for the remnant who are persecuted. Now, as of old, the blood of the martyrs is the seed of the Church. ✕ To-day, as yesterday, suffering alone gives the true faith—the key by which it can unlock the hearts of men. It must needs be that offences come, but it is not unto those by whom they come. When Colonel Pashkoff and Count Korff were exiled, they addressed a letter to the Emperor, in which this truth is set forth with much fidelity. They say:

"'The Lord's work in Russia will not be

✕ The behavior of the Russian Church was the sure-fire seed of Bolshevism.

hindered or stopped by our exile. What are, in
such a work, two persons like us? The Lord has
many servants who willingly follow His commands, and who are endowed more than we with
power and authority from Him. We are punished
innocently, but the Kingdom of God will grow
with still more power than before, for your good,
Sire, and for the good of our dear country. Our
undeserved exile will serve to consolidate this
work. Such an order from your government has
afflicted all the followers of Christ, but it has also
stimulated their zeal. The persecution, not only
of us, but also of books written with the sole object of giving men to understand the love of Christ
which passes our understanding—books which
are permitted by the Censure, and by Pobedonestzeff himself allowed to be spread abroad, when, in
the year 1880, they were seized in Nijni by Count
Ignatieff—such a persecution puts upon all the
servants of the Lord the duty of propagating
orally the knowledge of Christ more than they
did before. They try to persuade your Imperial
Majesty that the so-called Evangelical Sectarians
and Baptists are apostates who deny their native
land and people, who separate themselves from
everything Russian, who are rebels against the
supreme authority, and are advocates of the universal levelling of ranks. Allow us, Sire, to tell
you positively that such an opinion about them is
unjust. They are as much children of Russia as

the Orthodox ones; they love you as much as those do; they submit to the Tzar, not from fear, but for conscience's sake and from the desire to fulfil the will of God. Sire, allow us, your loyal subjects, who love you with the love of Christ, and who pray for you and for Russia, to implore you in the name of Christ: grant to Russia the supreme good which is in your power; make it lawful for every one to profess openly, and without hindrance, the hope in the Lord: recognize for us the right to believe as our conscience directs us; blot out all the punishments which are inflicted, equally with thieves and murderers, upon us who, for conscience's sake, leave the Orthodox Church; and then the blessing of the Lord, which is the most precious thing in the world, will be poured upon you, Sire, upon your Imperial family, and upon all Russia.'

"To that prayer no answer has yet been returned. The Orthodox seem to be in fear for the Church of the Living God if the Ispravnik is not ready with pains and penalties for those who, for conscience's sake, leave the Orthodox Church.

"For all such timorous ones, alike those who persecute from fear and those who dread lest that persecution may extinguish 'the spark of God' in the Russian Empire, I will conclude with a little apologue of Count Tolstoi's.

"'When I hear,' said he, 'that the Church is perishing, or going to perish, because of this, that,

or the other, that is being done by men in power,
it reminds me of the story of the boy and the
eagle. A little boy rushed one day into the
parlor to his father, crying excitedly, " Father, an
eagle, an eagle in the kitchen ! Come quickly
and rescue it, for the woman cook will not let it
go ! " And the father said, " Peace, my boy. If
it were really an eagle it would fly away, nor
could a woman cook stand for a moment in its
way. Believe me, it is only a hen." And when I
hear that the Church of Christ, which, if it exists at all, is real, eternal, spiritual, and Divine, is
going to perish because of what the government
is doing, I think of that eagle caged in the kitchen
by the woman cook, and I say to myself,
Peace, peace ; it is no eagle, it is only a hen ! '"

On the afternoon of this Sunday in St. Petersburg by appointment at the Hotel de Europe, we
received Lieutenant-General Alexander Kireef,
brother of Madame Olga Novikoff, the well-known
author upon Russia, of whom mention has already
been made when visiting at the Marble Palace.
General Kireef had fought all through the Plevna
campaign and the war in Bulgaria, and his stories
of the trials and difficulties in the Shipka Pass and
in the field with Skoboleef were as thrilling and
brilliant as Verestschagin's famous pictures upon
this subject in his well-known collection. Nothing, however, could exceed the modesty and
Christian gentleness of this bronzed and weather-

beaten soldier, who seemed to realize the apostle's
description of Cornelius the centurian as one who
was "just and devout and who served God with
all his house." General Kireef was a firm be-
liever in the possibility of Christian unity, by
which he meant a union of the Greek with the
Latin or Western Church. His lament over the
Filioque controversy was most honest and most
thorough, and his pious anticipation that the
Church of the future would wipe out the wrong
which had been done by omitting the disputed
expression was most interesting. He himself had
been a delegate to the Church conference held at
Bonn-upon-the-Rhine, and described to us his impressions of Dr. Dollinger of the Old Catholic
Church, and Bishop Young, the late Bishop of
Florida, who was the representative of the American Episcopal Church at this meeting. He had
a kind word to say for Pobedonestzeff, the much-
abused procurator of the Holy Synod. When we
talked with him about the tyrannies he had exercised as described by Mr. Stead, he smiled in
reply, and gave us to understand that Mr. Stead
has on hand an ample command of rhetoric. He
was very proud of his sister's books upon Russia,
and glowed with the ardor of a true-born soldier
over the brilliant but arrested career of the now
famous Skoboleef, whose life his sister had just
written in a book entitled "Skoboleef and the
Slavonic Cause." He gave us, in this afternoon's

interview, the Eastern question in a nut-shell. "The Slavs," he said, "will ultimately go to Russia. The Germans will go to Germany. Austria will disappear from among the nations of Europe and a network of dependent kingdoms will become federated around the headship of the Tzar as now in Germany the lesser German kingdoms are absorbed in the greater German Empire. Russia," he declared, "is the young giant among the nations. France and Spain and Italy and Germany and England have had their day. Their strength is in their past ; they are at present nations of history, but Russia is just beginning to assert her power. A literary, an artistic, a religious revival is each in its way bringing out hidden sources of power, and a process of assimilation of peoples will result, in the next century, in the development of a larger national unity than the Russia of to-day ever dreams of. All that has been in Germany and in England will appear in due time in Russia, whose period of reformation or age of renaissance is not as yet begun." General Kireef explained to us as it never had been brought home before, how it was that the unity which pervades Russia was a religious rather than a civil or secular unity. In addressing an audience, whether it be in Russia or in Bulgaria or in Servia or Roumania, the speaker would not begin with the expression " Ladies and gentlemen," or " Fellow-citizens," but would always strike deeper than this to that which was a central bond of unity, and would address the meeting by the well-known expression " My Fellow-Orthodox." General Kireef, while admiring Tolstoi, had little faith in his schemes of reform, and thought that Tolstoi in a certain way was extemporizing in his own individual fashion upon the revelation of Jesus Christ, very much as Richard Wagner allegorized the music of his operas from the old legends of the German fatherland.

We parted from our kind and genial military friend in the evening, and after writing our letters home that night, sent for Pilley and made out our plans for the morrow.

Too bad Dr Newton's vision was not more prophetic. Blind "Orthodox" like General Kireef were the forerunners of — Christ? No! — LENIN ti whom Christ (because of the Russian Church) was anathema!

CHAPTER V.

THE three American travellers took the night train for Moscow at 8:30 o'clock. Mr. Pilley procured the tickets for the party, and after a farewell caution about not getting left over at the railway stopping-places, waved his hat, after the manner of Napoleon at Austerlitz, and we saw him no more.

Hereupon Lord Byron fell into a fit of prolonged philosophizing about the advantage which would accrue if it were possible to have a James Pilley go through life for one—making the hard places smooth and the rough places plain ; explaining every thing on the tourist view of life, and overcoming all nascent and expressed difficulties by usurping one's own feeble will with his own all-wise dominant determination to bring things through. Lord Byron always talked, while travelling through Russia, in a subdued and humming-bird character of voice, finally ending in a stage whisper, for fear of the secret police force of the third section ; so that much of his valuable conversation became hopelessly lost, and in this way—like the explorers of Nineveh and the ruins of Zoan—we are able to reconstruct but a portion of his proverbial philosophy.

But Mr. Pilley's warning was not in vain. A most alarming tendency developed itself on the part of Mr. Thackeray and Lord Byron, to get out at way-stations on the road and proceed with steady tread to the buffet to refresh the inner man exhausted by too much Winter Palace and Hermitage, and lunches with the Russian nobility.

Warnings being in vain, it became necessary for the third member of the party to learn the Russian word for " all on board," and having told them in advance just what it was, to sound it in their ears as they sat by the open window of the buffet and, in this way, to enforce a speedy retreat to the train. This train for Moscow moved along on a double track, quite like the heavy movement of a Pullman drawing-room car on the New York Central or Pennsylvania railroad, and by 10 o'clock the following day the domes and turrets of the four hundred churches in Moscow came in sight.

There are three great sights to see in Moscow, viz., the city itself, the Kremlin, and St. Saviour's Church.

St. Petersburg, with its dashing droskies driving along the Nevskoi Prospekt, seemed like old Rome, with its chariots driving along the stony streets of the Imperial City, where now is the Corso.

Moscow, at once, with its Kremlin towers and wall, so strikingly painted in Verestchagin's famous picture in his collection of Russian paintings, seemed like Jerusalem in the days of King Herod, when there came wise men from the East to worship the Infant King of the Jews.

St. Petersburg seems a Western and a European city—Moscow is essentially Eastern and Muscovitish.

The following brief description of the history of Moscow is taken from the interesting pages of Murray:

"In the fourteenth century Moscow became the capital of Muscovy; Kief, and afterwards Vladimir, having till then enjoyed that distinction. In the early part of the reign of Basil II. it was taken and ravaged by Tamerlane; and later it fell again into the hands of the Tartars, who sacked it, and put many of the inhabitants to the sword. In 1536 the town was nearly consumed by fire, in which 2,000 of the inhabitants perished. In 1572 the Tartars fired the suburbs and, a furious wind driving the flames into the city, a considerable portion of it was reduced to ashes, and no fewer than 100,000 persons perished in the flames or by the sword. In 1611 a great portion of the city was again destroyed by fire, when the Poles had taken possession of it, under the pretence of defending the inhabitants from the adherents of a pretender to the crown. The plague of 1771 diminished the population by several thousands—a decrease from which it has never recovered. And, lastly, in 1812, the Muscovites gave up their ancient, holy and beautiful city to the devouring element—the grandest sacrifice ever made to national feeling. The city was the idol of every Russian's heart, her shrines were to him the holiest in the empire—hallowed by seven centuries of historical associations."

But we have to describe the city as it is, rather than to revert to Russian history. The assertion sometimes made, that no city is so irregularly built as Moscow, is in some respects true ; none of the streets are straight ; houses large and small, public buildings, churches and other edifices are mingled confusedly together; but it gains by this the advantage of being more picturesque. The streets undulate continually, and thus offer from time to time points of view whence the eye is able to range over the vast ocean of house-tops, trees and gilded and colored domes. The profusion of churches, 370 in number, is a characteristic feature of the city. But the architecture of Moscow, since the conflagration of 1812, is not quite so bizarre as, according to the accounts of travellers, it was before that event ; nevertheless it is singular enough. In 1813 the point chiefly in view was to build, and build quickly, rather than to carry any certain plan into execution ; the houses were replaced with nearly the same irregularity with respect to each other, and the streets became as crooked and tortuous as before. The whole gained, therefore, little in regularity from the fire, but each individual house was built in much better taste, gardens became more frequent, the majority of roofs were made of iron, painted green, a lavish use was made of pillars, and even those who could not be profuse erected more elegant cottages.

Hence Moscow has all the charms of a new city, with the pleasing negligence and picturesque irregularity of an old one. In the streets we come now to a large magnificent palace, with all the pomp of Corinthian pillars, wrought-iron trellis-work and magnificent approaches and gateways ; and now to a simple whitewashed house, the abode of a modest citizen's family. Near them stands a small church, with green cupolas and golden stars. Then comes a row of little yellow wooden houses, and these are succeeded by one of the new colossal public institutions. Sometimes the road winds through a number of little streets, and the traveller might fancy himself in a country town ; suddenly it rises, and he is in a wide "place," from which streets branch off on all sides, while the eye wanders over the forest of houses of the great capital ; descending again, he comes in the middle of the town to the banks of the river. The circumvallation of the city is

upwards of twenty English miles in extent, of
a most irregular form, more resembling a trape-
zium than any other figure ; within this are two
nearly concentric circular lines of boulevards,
the sites of former fortifications, the one at a
distance of about one mile and a half from the
Kremlin, completed on both sides of the Moskva ;
the internal one—once the moat of the Kremlin
and Kitai Gorod—with a radius of about a mile,
spreading only on the north of the river, and
terminating near the stone bridge on the one
side, and the Foundling Hospital on the other.
The river enters the barrier of the vast city to
which it has given a name about the central point
of the western side; and after winding around the
Devichi convent like a serpent, and from thence
flowing beneath the battlements of the Kremlin,
and receiving the scanty stream of the Jaousa,
issues again into the vast plain, till it meets the
Oka, a tributary of the mighty Volga, which it
joins at Nijni Novgorod.

On the north of the Moskva, streets and houses,
in regular succession, reach to the very barrier ;
and though a vast proportion of ground is left
unoccupied, owing to the enormous width of the
streets and boulevards, the earthen rampart may
truly be said to gird in the city. But in the other
quarters, and particularly to the south, Moscow
can hardly be said to extend further than the
outward boulevard.

The centre of this vast collection of buildings
is the Kremlin, which forms nearly a triangle of
about two English miles in extent.   On the east
comes the Kitai Gorod (Chinese city), which still
preserves its ancient fence of towers and but-
tresses.   Encircling these two divisions, and itself
bounded by the river and inner boulevard, lies
the Beloi Gorod (white city).   The space enclosed
between the two circles to the north of the
Moskva, and between the river and the outward
boulevard on the south, is called the Zemlianoi
Gorod.   Beyond the boulevards are the suburbs.

Before entering the Kremlin it will be well to
view it from one or two points on the outside, and
the most favorable spot for this purpose, on the
south side, is the stone bridge across the Moskva ;
from the river that washes its base the hill of the
Kremlin rises, picturesquely adorned with turf
and shrubs.   The buildings appear set in a rich
frame of water, verdant foliage, and snowy wall,
the majestic column of Ivan Veliki rearing itself
high above all, like the axis round which the whole
moves.   The colors everywhere are most lively
—red, white, green, gold and silver.   Amidst the
confusion of the numerous small antique edifices,
the Bolshoi Dvorets (the large palace built by
Nicholas) has an imposing aspect.

After visiting the many strange and interesting
sights in the Kremlin, this party of three—with no
Pilley to conduct one's way and manage one's

thinking—sat for a long time under the spacious dome of St. Saviour's Church and watched the incessant procession of monks, peasant women, soldiers and Russian field laborers, who, with their muskrat faces, sheep-skin coverings, felt boots and all-pervasive smell of leather, filed in and out of this greatest Temple of the Eastern Church.

And some such train of thought as this forced its way into the writer's mind. Moscow is to the Europe of to-day something like that which Prague was three centuries ago. This wilderness of spires, belonging to four hundred churches, marks it as an Eastern and an Asiatic city. Yet this Eastern religion is thoroughly provincial ; there is nothing large or cosmopolitan about it. The troubled face of St. John the Divine and the grieved look of Peter, in the famous picture of "The Last Supper," behind the Metropolitan's throne in this St. Saviour's Church, are reproduced to-day in the thoughtful minds of all sincere Russian Christians, as they feel in their inmost souls that after all that can be said, their Church has betrayed the simple Jesus of the Gospels for the state Christ of the Orthodox Church, which church is only an arm of the government.—like the army or the navy or the third section of the secret police.

Moscow is the border city between Europe and Asia. The East and the West will meet here some day. The American Alaska, with steamer and railroad termination, will force a way into the heart of Europe via the Russian Empire, and then the provincialism of Russia will be a thing of the past.*

The East will meet the West and will take on at last the stirring active features of its civilization ; the West will learn from this Eastern empire something of its reserve and rugged strength, and the coming man will be the third term in the problem, the product of these two natural forces.

But our plain and pragmatical guide—a mere tertiary deposit or a base Silurian compared with the omniscient Pilley—called us from our reveries to see more sights in the way of churches, palaces, museums and untold memorabilia, the accounts of which are written in the prolific pages of " Murray " and " Bædeker."

In the afternoon of this same day this party hired a carriage, and after driving through the city, brought up at last with a sort of round turn dramatic effect at the house of Count Tolstoi, as the chariot of the Syrian rumbled its wheels to the door of the Prophet Elisha—a prophet in each case being the object of search. We found a quiet, old-fashioned stone and plaster house, inside of a walled enclosure, very much like a walled

---

*Since this sentence has been penned a graphic and detailed account has gone the rounds of the American press, describing a proposed plan for a railroad through Alaska to Behring Straits, with a tunnel under the straits connecting with a railway from the Russian coast to Moscow and thence by Moscow to Berlin.

French château, such as one sees constantly in France and Belgium, in pictures and engravings of the scenes of '93, with the *emigrés* homes as the base of the story. Our letters from the Tolstoi family, at the Winter Palace in St. Petersburg, secured for us a warm reception, and before we knew it the children and the English governess and some young lady guests were chatting away in excellent English as if we were very much at home. The Count's family had heard of our proposed visit and had notified him of our coming. He was away on a visit, fifteen miles beyond the monastery town of Troitsa, which is about forty miles by rail from Moscow. A certain Russian friend, named Prince Ourouzeff, had urged Count Tolstoi to visit him on his farm, and he was at this time making his visit. Still, he had left word that if his unknown American friends should come all this distance to see him, they should be helped on their way for the rest of their journey, and push on until they found him at his hospitable old friend's mansion.

So the sweet and obliging daughter sent a telegram in that most undecipherable Russian language, to the effect that we would leave at 6 o'clock the next morning, and would be at Troitsa at 10 o'clock. And after bidding our friends good-bye, we went home to the hotel, to be prepared to leave on the morrow for the visit to Count Tolstoi.

It seemed to us then, on that drosky ride to the hotel, that it was not such a fool's errand after all. We were like soldiers at the front, who were to make the attack upon the morrow. What would the end be? How would Count Tolstoi meet us? He looked in his pictures like a fierce sort of Russian Thomas Carlyle. Would he knock us down metaphorically, like Giant Despair with his crab-apple cudgel belaboring his captives in Doubting Castle—only on purpose to set us up again for a second playful game of metaphysical ten-pins?

"How very far away we are from home," sighed Lord Byron, as the third member of the party went into a Moscow apothecary's to hunt for a Russian Alcock's Porous Plaster to forfend the rumbling threatenings of some rheumatic twinges.

"Far away from home, did you say?" replied his friend, on emerging from the store. "Not a bit of it; look here! What do you think I have found on the shelf of this Russian drug store?" and the third term in the party produced from his pocket a bottle of "Mother Siegel's Carminative Syrup," made at the Shaker establishment, on the way to Lebanon Springs—six miles from Pittsfield, Massachusetts—and decocted in the laboratory of his old friend, Brother Alonzo Hollister, whose photograph the writer had often shown to strangers as a picture of "Emerson upon his farm."

CHAPTER VI.

THE train from Moscow to the famous monastery town of Troitsa left the station at 6:30 in
the morning, and the day was a Russian day,
cold and gray and leaden.

At 9:30 we found ourselves at Troitsa, where,
while the tritska was being made ready, we wan-
dered through this ancient and strong-smelling
town. Fat and pudgy vegetarian monks abounded
on all sides; we counted nearly four hundred
that morning in the refectory and at chapel and
in the various apartments of their famous monastery. These monks seemed so like soft dough or
putty, that one was almost tempted to pull their
fat cheeks to twist them into shape, as the boys
do with the gutta-percha faces which are pulled
and twisted into all sorts of shapes and forms.

"Troitsa," as Murray says, "is the Canterbury
of Russia," and a day may well be devoted to it.
St. Sergius, the son of a boyar of Rostof, at the
head of twelve disciples, established a monastery
on this spot about the year 1342. His piety and
the honor conferred upon him by the Patriarch of
Constantinople soon rendered him and his brother-

hood famous. The princes of Moscow sought his
counsel and the oft-mentioned Dimitry of the
Don was blessed by him before he set out for the
battle of Kulikova. Two monks from this monastery, Osliabia and Peresvest, fought by the
side of the victorious prince, and one of them
fell dead, together with his Tartar adversary in
single combat. The intervention of St. Sergius
on this memorable occasion was rewarded by
large grants of lands, and thenceforth the monastery grew rich and powerful; its abbot, however,
the holy Sergius, remaining, as before, simple,
self-denying and laborious, and cutting wood and
fetching water to the last. His right to canoniza-
tion was still further established by the visitation
(recorded in the annals of the Russo-Greek
Church) of the Holy Virgin, who appeared in his
cell, accompanied by the Apostles Peter and
John, about the year 1388. He died in 1392.
The Tartar hordes of Khan Edigei laid waste
this holy habitation in 1408, and it was only
re-established, together with the present Cathedral of the Holy Trinity, in 1423. Thirty monasteries were subsequently attached to it, and much
land, until, in 1764, St. Sergius was the possessor
as well as the patron of more than 106,000 male
serfs. The most prominent portion of the history of the monastery is the siege by 30,000 Poles
under Sapieha and Lisofski in 1608, which was
only raised after sixteen months, on the approach

of a large Russian force. Later again, after the election of Michael Romanoff, Ladislaus of Poland, styling himself Tzar of Muscovy, besieged the Troitsa monastery once more, but he was repulsed by the brotherhood. When the Poles were in possession of Moscow, the monks of St. Sergius rendered considerable assistance to their countrymen in the shape of supplies in bread and money. The most interesting fact, however, in the records of the Troitsa monastery is that it was the place of refuge on two occasions of Peter the Great and his brother John when they fled from the insurgent Streltsi. Since then the repose of the monks has not been disturbed by political events. The French, in 1812, went half-way towards the monastery, but returned without the expected booty.

The plague and the cholera have never ventured within the holy walls, which were founded in 1513 and finished in 1547. They extend 4,500 feet and are from thirty to fifty feet high, with a thickness of twenty feet. They were put in order by Peter the Great, but their present appearance is due to a later period. Eight towers form the angles; one of them, of Gothic architecture, is surmounted by an obelisk, terminating in a duck carved in stone, to commemorate the fact of Peter the Great having practised duck-shooting on a neighboring pond.

There are ten churches within the monastery.

The most ancient is the Cathedral of Trinity. The shrine of St. Sergius stands within it, weighing 936 pounds of pure silver. The relics of the saint are exposed to view. In the altar-screen, in a glass case, will be seen the staff and other ecclesiastical appurtenances of the patron. Two pictures of the saint, painted on portions of his coffin, are suspended on the walls. That near the shrine was carried into battle by the Tzar Alexis and by Peter the Great ; and the Emperor Alexander I. was blessed with it in 1812. On a silver plate, at the back of the image, are recorded the several military occasions at which it assisted. The interior of the cathedral is replete with massive silver ornaments, and in the archbishop's stall is a representation of the Last Supper, of which the figures are of solid gold, with the exception of Judas, who is of brass. All the images are adorned with precious stones. The small chapel alongside was added in 1552, rebuilt in 1623, and again in 1779 and 1840. Next to this is a small chapel erected over the supposed site of the cell in which the Holy Virgin appeared to St. Sergius. The large church, with five cupolas, was consecrated in 1585 and is called the Assumption of the Virgin. The frescoes were painted in 1681. One of its altars was consecrated in 1609, during the roar of the Polish artillery, and devoted to prayer for deliverance from the scurvy, of which disease three thousand of the inmates of the monastery had already perished.

The large two-headed eagle in wood commemorates the concealment of Peter the Great under ∨ the altar during the insurrection of the Streltsi.

Off the southwest angle of the church is a well dug by St. Sergius and discovered in 1644, at a time when the monastery was in great need of fresh water. Between the Assumption and the belfry stands a monument erected in 1792, on which the principal events in the history of the monastery are recorded.

The fourth church, " The Descent of the Holy Ghost," was founded after the capture of Kazan by the Tzar Ivan Vassilevitch in person. The tomb of Maximus, a learned Greek, stands in a small chapel close by. The next church in importance is that of " Sergius Radonejeski," with an immense refectory and a gallery all round, built in 1692. The iron roof, added in 1746 after a fire, is of a very peculiar mechanical construction. Over the church is a depository of nearly four thousand old books and manuscripts, amongst the most remarkable of which is a copy of the Evangelists on parchment, attributed to the early part of the thirteenth century.

Four hundred monks were surging in and out the buildings of this crowded monastery, while all the time the squalor and misery and wretchedness of the village with dreary-looking hamlets and broken carts and dilapidated-looking children and cattle told the story of monastic inefficiency to remedy this existing state of misery which a New England town-meeting would regulate in a week's time.

After visiting this interesting but very dirty monastery town, a three-horse sledge was obtained, and with a guide to accompany us the sledge started forth in the direction of the Russian nobleman's manor house. But how little does the average man and the average travelling man know what is in store for him when he riseth up early and goeth forth cheerily to a day's unforeseen excursion. We had not gone far before there followed a series of accidents.

The traces broke ; snow-drifts, mud, rivulets of water, and piles of rubbish blocked the way ; and the driver and the guide, after no little consultation, decided that it was impossible to proceed. At this juncture a Muscovite peasant, with a banged head of hair and a typical muskrat face, appeared upon the rutty road and informed us that Prince Ourouzeff was expecting a party of Americans and had sent a couple of sledges to meet them half a verst further on. And thus, in an hour's time from the moment we left the rejected and deserted sledge, we were welcomed at the Russian manor house by two strangers, one a tall and square-faced gentleman, and the other a diminutive and sensitive-looking man.

The tall stranger with the silvery head was Prince Ourouzeff; and the gentle-mannered man, more poet than artist or reformer, was the famous Count Leo Tolstoi, soldier, society-man, novelist, religious reformer and radical all in one.

But the difficulties of this journey to Prince Ourouzeff's can never be rightly detailed. The dreary pathway across a desert which was a prairie with no fences or trees save bushes and scrub-oak ; the war of the elements, when all the powers invoked in the Benedicite seemed to make their appearance that day—fire and heat, mist and vapor, ice and snow and all the winds of God ; the broken sledge ; the spiritless horses ; the dejected pedestrians ; the disconsolate guide ; the rebellious and mutinous companions ; the would-be Columbus, not heeding the mutterings and curses of his fellow-voyagers and keeping well in advance out of ear-shot of their revilings —all made the appearance of the messenger from the manor house of Prince Ourouzeff seem like the slogan of Havelock's Campbells at Lucknow, or the shrill whistle of the steamer " Thetis " to the Greely survivors at Camp Clay among the Greenland icebergs.

Mr. Thackeray and Lord Byron were together in one sledge in the rear, while the guide and the other member of the party went on in advance in these Russian semi-canal boats drawn by a stout horse apiece, with a peasant driver in attendance. Whenever the writer looked back at his companions coming on behind through the mud and slush of this aqueous route, Lord Byron could be seen with upraised hands—after the manner of Buddha under the Bo tree—as if the joined thumbs and perpendicular digitals indicated a degree of amazement for which no choice of words was adequate. But in an evil moment, as Lord Byron, with closed eyes and upraised hands, was communing with his inward or astral body, his sledge gave a lurch, and our poetical friend was tipped out into a soft, wet, yellow patch of mud, where, in his abject helplessness, he continued sitting with upraised hands and closed eyes, despite the fact that his companion, Mr. Thackeray, with rope and stick and a rudimentary vocabulary of the Russian tongue, was vainly suggesting to the stolid Muscovitish driver that the proper thing to be done was to replace the rapt and transcendental poet upon the thwart of their semi-canal boat again. Was it any wonder that, in the subsequent interview with Count Tolstoi and his friend, our host, Lord Byron should find his mind diverted from the object of this pilgrimage to the miserable condition of his apparel, and that he should emulate the tactics of the Apostle of old and seek to warm himself by the crackling fire which played upon Prince Ourouzeff's generous hearth? A lunch followed, and an afternoon and evening were spent together wandering around the Rus-

sian farm. Our talk was about war, politics, literature, religion, the evils of civilization and the need
above everything else of the return of Christianity
to the literalism of Jesus. This man is sincere
and true ; he is radical and one-sided ; he has
been very unwise in his latest story—written
since this visit—in thinking aloud in French and
Russian in a vein not allowable in English type
and ink.

Perhaps, by this time, with all the awful conditions that are about him, he is a bit crazed in
his outlook upon life. But then Tolstoi is the
voice in the wilderness in Russia to-day ; and
when the new Russia is evolved out of her social,
political, literary and religious House of Bondage,
the name of Tolstoi—not as the author of " Anna
Karènina," or the " Kreutzer Sonata," but as the
author of " My Confession," and " My Religion "
—will be remembered as the prophet of this
period of Russian renaissance ; just as Dante is
remembered to-day in Italy, or Luther is not forgotten in the German fatherland.*

---

* That the teachings of Tolstoi are beginning at last to have a distinct following is seen from the subjoined dispatch to a Boston newspaper of the date of October 29th, 1890 :

FOLLOWERS OF TOLSTOI.

*The Theories of the Novelist put in practice by Russian Ladies and
Gentlemen.*

BERLIN, Oct. 28. A curious experiment is being made at Vishne-
volot, Uzmi, in the government of Tver, Russia, by the admirers of
Count Tolstoi, who have formed themselves into an association and
propose carrying his theories into practice. They are all ladies and
gentlemen of the upper classes, but have donned the peasant costume,
and live simple, industrious lives.

CHAPTER VII.

A BOSTON newspaper describes a discussion recently held concerning Count Tolstoi as follows: "At a meeting of the Unitarian Club, at the Hotel Vendome, in Boston, Mr. Joseph Lee made a long and interesting address upon the personality and theories of Count Tolstoi. As Mr. Lee had visited the great Russian novelist and philosopher at his home, he had had peculiar opportunities for observation and learning the causes which had led to his opinions. Mr. Lee thought that Tolstoi had reached his conclusions rather by instinct than by close reasoning, as it seemed to him that Tolstoi lacked mental training, is impatient of argument, and does not think systematically.

Other speakers followed with an interesting discussion ; Rev. Dr. Peabody taking the ground that it was high time for the country to hear the gospel of simplicity. Prof. Sedgwick, of the Institute of Technology, said, "To adopt Tolstoi's views would reduce all people to the level of the cave-dwellers." He refused to have him set up for a guide.

There are three things to be considered when we come to study out the story of Count Tolstoi's life, and these are, what he has written, what he has done, and what he is. The social, religious, artistic, literary, and political forces of the Russia of the present day form a study which taxes the bravest and most enthusiastic enquirer.

In the midst of barbaric splendor and squalor, in the very presence of imperial autocracy on the one hand, and nihilistic strivings on the other hand, Count Leo Tolstoi—soldier, novelist, and social leader—returns, as by the preaching of a John the Baptist in the wilderness, to the literalism of the words of Christ, and shows the power once more in the world's history of the principle of renunciation, as Buddha showed it in India, and the Divine founder of Christianity showed it in Galilee and Judea, and as George Fox and William Penn have exhibited it in the sensuous and luxurious age of the dissolute Charles II.

In a notice of Dr. George Brandes' recent work, entitled, "Impressions of Russia," a reviewer in *The New York Churchman* writes as follows : " The attention of the age is fixed upon the Russian people and the Russian empire. Not only is the latter the most important factor in European politics, but the former is the most interesting study among nationalities. Politically, the Russian empire is the x of the European equation, and the algebriac puzzle is to know

what sign, whether plus or minus, is to be prefixed
to it. We have used the terms Russian empire
and Russian people advisedly, because one great
feature in this uncertainty lies in the fact that
the empire is a great power imposed upon the
people. It sits like Sinbad's old man of the sea,
astride the shoulders of the nation. Everywhere
else in Europe there is a certain correspondence
between government and nation, something of
mutuality, if it be but a tradition of growth and
development. But in Russia there is nothing of
the sort. Even the blood of the Romanoff
dynasty is nine-tenths German, and yet the passion of that dynasty has been almost entirely to
wage war against Western civilization. In other
lands rank is the symbol, somewhat, of separation.
The English peer, who looks back to Battle Abbey
roll and Doomsday Book ; the French noble, who
cherishes the pre-revolutionary memories of a
house dating back to the Crusades ; the German,
who cherishes his sixteen quarterings as more
precious than land or wealth; all these belong to
a patrician class and are conscious of a distinction
which the *roturier* cannot attain. But in Russia
there is no such feeling. There is no antiquity
to which the Russian looks back. Rank is mainly
bureaucratic, given or taken away, at the pleasure
of the crown. Birth and lineage go for very little. Wealth and power are all in all. While the
Russian obeys with a submission which is Orien-

tal, Asiatic in its fond humility, it is simply because such seems to him the order of the universe.
He submits as he submits to the sun which warms
him or the frost that chills him, because he has no
idea that he can change the operation of heat
or cold.

"Yet in this Russian people there is a great
power, a vast, undeveloped capacity, and it is this
Russian Empire that is striving with the one hand
to use, and with the other to repress, the native
talent and energy. It is this spectacle which
makes Russia a study at once painful and fascinating, and Russian literature, as the true exponent
of the various phases and workings of the popular
nature, the most deeply interesting literature of
the day. Elsewhere, men and women who write,
belong, whatever their nationality, to the Catholic
Church of the republic of letters ; they owe a
certain fealty to literature at large. But the Russian writer is the representative of his people,
and all that is of worth in his work comes directly
from the thoughts and feelings which are throb-
bing in the brain and heart of that people.

"We have briefly given, in the above statement
the impression which this book, which we have
read with intense interest, has made upon us.
It is the work of a highly-cultured and acute
observer and most fair-minded critic. In the
first part, Dr. Brandes has told us of the way in
which Russia appears to him ; in the second, he

has given a brief, but very striking, outline of Russian literature. The two things go together as nowhere else in the world. That hidden future, which so inscrutably broods over the vast Empire stretching from the German frontier to the Pacific shore, is dimly prophesied in the pages of Russia's authors, and the fires which smoulder beneath the surface and are held down by the gigantic forces of the Empire burn the more vividly through the loopholes which a relentless censorship overlooks. No· novel we ever read has more of fascination than a well-written book on Russia, because no fiction can approach that strangest medley of power and weakness, which bears the name of Muscovite."

The story of Count Tolstoi's life is the story of the growth of a soul. There is almost nothing of outward incident in his life that could excite the interest of the reader. His has been a life of thought, of spiritual aspiration, struggle and vision, combined with the most laborious art. It is, therefore, a story incapable of anything approaching to dramatic treatment. It were impossible to give life and movement to a narrative constructed out of "My Confession," and· "My Religion," and these works contain the account of his own spiritual development, aside from which his life-story is barren of interest.

Count Lyof Nikolaevitch Tolstoi was born August 28, 1828, in the village of Yasnaya Poly-

ana, his mother's estate, in the Department of
Tula. He was of aristocratic lineage, his father
being a direct descendant of Count Piotr Andree-
vitch, an attendant at the Court of Peter the
Great. His mother was the only daughter of
Prince Nikolai Sergieevitch Volkonsky.

Thus, like most of his illustrious predecessors in
the field of Russian literature—Lomonosof and
Dostoyevski being notable exceptions—he was
of noble birth and patrician education. The fact
that literature in Russia has been the favorite,
almost exclusively, of the aristocratic and educated classes, has contributed not a little to the
high standard of literary art and the purity of
taste among her writers. Lomonosof had little
art and less taste. Dostoyevski, although a great
author, was deficient in artistic skill, and his taste
was often bad. It was the high-born writers—
Pushkin, Lermontof, Turgenief, Tolstoi—who set
a standard of taste and artistic achievement
unattained in point of purity and power by the
literature of any other people.

Of Tolstoi's childhood we know nothing,
except what may be dimly gathered from his first
published work, a novel, entitled " Childhood "—
followed later by " Boyhood " and " Youth "—in
which the leading incidents and chief characteris-
tics of his own early life are doubtless reflected.
In 1830, before he had reached the age of two
years, his mother died, leaving him and three

elder brothers and a younger sister to be educated under the supervision of a distant relative, Tatyna Alexandrovna Yergolskaya by name, whose memory is warmly cherished in the Tolstoi family.

The education of the young Tolstoi was no small undertaking, even for a woman of character and culture, and seems to have been attended with considerable vexation. The work of instruction was committed, in the main, to tutors ; some German, some French, some Russian, none of whom were retained through any very lengthened term of service. His love for his German teacher and his hatred for the Frenchman who succeeded him fill a large space in his " Childhood." So far as can be inferred from the same source, he was at that time a healthy, sensitive and extravagantly imaginative child, with a good deal of pride, and morbidly sensible of his homely flat nose and thick lips.

The family continued to reside in the country until 1837, when the entrance of the eldest son in the university seemed to ·render advisable the removal of the entire family to Moscow. Scarcely had they established themselves there when the father suddenly died, leaving his affairs in great confusion. A paternal aunt, the Countess Alexandra Ilinitchna Osten-Saken, was appointed guardian of the young Tolstois and decided at once, from motives of economy, to leave the two elder children in Moscow and take the other three, together with the ever-devoted Tatyana Yergolskaya, into the country, where their education was looked after in a desultory and uncertain way by various tutors.

In 1840 the guardian of the Tolstoi children, the Countess Osten-Saken, died, and the guardianship devolved upon another paternal aunt, who, with her husband, lived in Kazan. Thither all the young Tolstois were removed in 1841, the eldest being transferred, at his guardian's request, from the university of Moscow to that of Kazan. Here, after two years' preparation, the young Count Lyof Nikolaevitch entered the university in 1843 at the age of fifteen. At this point the memoirs contained in "Youth" become less interesting, furnishing the inference that his life as a student was not different from the ordinary monotony of existence in Russian universities before the days of nihilistic plots. His first interest in religious questions had begun shortly before, about a year after his first removal to Moscow. Of this he gives the following account in his "Confession" :

"I remember once in my twelfth year, a boy now long since dead, Vladimir M—, a pupil in a gymnasium, spent a Sunday with us and brought us the news of the last discovery in the gymnasium, namely : that there was no God, and that all we were taught on this subject was a mere

invention (this was in 1838). I remember well
how interested my elder brothers were in this
news. I was admitted to their deliberations, and
we all eagerly accepted the theory as something
particularly attractive and possibly quite true.
I remember, also, that when my elder brother
Demetry, then at the university, with the impul-
siveness natural to his character, gave himself up
to a passionate faith, began to attend the church
services regularly, to fast, and to lead a pure and
moral life, we all of us, and some older than ourselves, never ceased to hold him up to ridicule,
and for some incomprehensible reason gave him
the nickname of Noah. I remember that Mous-
sin Poushkin, the then curator of the University
of Kazan, having invited us to a ball, tried to
persuade my brother, who had refused the invitation, by the jeering argument that even ' David
danced before the Ark.'

" I sympathized then with these jokes of my
elders, and drew from them this conclusion: that
I was bound to learn my catechism and to go to
church, but that it was not necessary to think of
my religious duties more seriously. I also
remember that I read Voltaire when I was very
young, and that his tone of mockery amused
without disgusting me. The gradual estrange-
ment from all belief went on in me as it does and
always has done in those of the same social position and culture."

The young Tolstoi spent a year in the division of Oriental languages, after which he passed to the department of jurisprudence, where he remained two years. At the end of that time he suddenly resolved to leave the university without completing his course. This resolution seems to have been due to a fresh desire for the country life of his childhood, aroused by the preparations of his brother for departure to the country home at Yasnaya Polyana, after having passed the final examinations.

No entreaties or arguments—even when used by the rector and professors of the university—were powerful enough to dissuade him from this course, and accordingly to Yasnaya Polyana, which had fallen to him in the division of his father's estates, he went, in the spring of 1846.

Here, for the next five years, his life furnished no material for the biographer. He lived uninterruptedly in the country until 1851. What his mental occupations were, whether he wrote anything during this period, or when the instinct of authorship first seized him, is altogether unknown.

At the age of twenty-three he quitted the estate and accompanied his brother to the Caucasus, where the latter had been serving in the Junker's corps. He was entirely captivated by the wild charms of this rugged and picturesque region, as well as by the new type of humanity which he found there, and resolved to enter the service, and accordingly joined the same battery with his brother. It is probable that the literary impulse first attacked him here, under the inspiration of his romantic surroundings, for it is certain that his first published work—a novel under the title of "Childhood"—was written during this period. Besides, he also wrote at this time "The Cossacks," so much admired by Turgenief, "The Incursion," and "The Felling of the Forest."

For two years he served in the Caucasus as a common soldier, after which, on the outbreak of the Crimean war, he was transferred, at his own request, to the army of the Danube. Here he served in the campaign of 1854 on the staff of Prince Gortchakoff. Going afterwards to Sevastopol, he was made commander of a division. During this period he began those wonderfully vivid descriptions of military life which first made him famous as a writer. "Military Tales" was succeeded by "Sevastopol in May" and "Sevastopol in December."

In 1855 Count Tolstoi went on the retired list, and entered actively on his renowned and brilliant career as a writer. "Youth," "Sevastopol in August," "Two Hussars," "Three Deaths," "Family Happiness," and "Polikuschka," appeared in rapid succession, and raised him at once to the foremost rank among authors. Concerning his life in those years, he speaks as follows in " My Confession " :

"I cannot now recall those years without a painful feeling of horror and loathing. I put men to death in war, I fought duels to slay others, I lost at cards, wasted my substance wrung from the sweat of peasants, punished the latter cruelly, rioted with loose women, and deceived men. Lying, robbery, adultery of all kinds, drunkenness, violence, and murder, all committed by me, not one crime omitted, and yet I was not the less considered by my equals a comparatively moral man. Such was my life during ten years.

"During that time I began to' write, out of vanity, love of gain, and pride. I followed as a writer the same path which I had chosen as a man. In order to obtain the fame and the money for which I wrote, I was obliged to hide what was good and bow down before what was evil. How often, while writing, have I cudgeled my brains to conceal under the mask of indifference or pleasantry those yearnings for something better, which formed the real problem of my life ! I succeeded in my object and was praised. At twenty-six years of age, on the close of the war, I came to St. Petersburg and made the acquaintance of the authors of the day. I met with a hearty reception and much flattery.

"Before I had time to look around, the prejudices and views of life common to the writers

of the class with which I associated became my
own, and completely put an end to all my former
struggles after a better life. These views, under
the influence of the dissipation into which I had
plunged, issued in a theory of life which justified
it. The view of life taken by these my fellow-
writers was, that life is a development, and the
principal part in that development is played by
ourselves, the thinkers, while among the thinkers
the chief influence is again due to ourselves, the
poets. Our vocation is to teach mankind.

"In order to avoid answering the very natural
question, 'What do I know, and what can I teach?'
the theory in question is made to contain the
formula that such is not required to be known,
but that the thinker and the poet teach unconsciously. I was myself considered a marvellous
littérateur and poet, and I, therefore, very naturally adopted this theory. Meanwhile, thinker and
poet though I was, I wrote and taught I knew
not what. For doing this I received large sums
of money. I kept a splendid table, had an excellent lodging, associated with loose women, and
received my friends handsomely ; moreover, I had
fame. It would seem, then, that what I taught
must have been good ; the faith in poetry and the
development of life was a true faith, and I was
one of its high priests, a post of great importance
and of profit. I long remained in this belief, and
never once doubted its truth.

" In the second, however, and especially in the third year of this way of life, I began to doubt the infallibility of the doctrine, and to examine it more closely. The first doubtful fact which attracted my attention was that the apostles of this belief did not agree among themselves. They disputed, quarrelled, abused, deceived and cheated one another. Moreover, there were many among us who, quite indifferent to right or wrong, only cared for their own private interests. All this forced on me doubts as to the truth of our belief. Again, when I doubted this faith in the influence of literary men, I began to examine more closely into the character and conduct of its chief professors, and I convinced myself that these writers were men who led immoral lives, most of them worthless and insignificant individuals, and far beneath the moral level of those with whom I had associated during my former dissipated and military career ; these men, however, had none the less an amount of self-confidence only to be expected in those who are conscious of being saints, or in those for whom holiness is an empty name.

" I grew disgusted with mankind and with myself, and I understood that this belief which I had accepted was a delusion. The strangest thing in all this was that though I soon saw the falseness of this belief and renounced it, I did not renounce the position I had gained by it ; I still called myself a thinker, a poet, and a teacher. I was simple enough to imagine that I, the poet and thinker, was able to teach other men without knowing myself what it was that I attempted to teach. I had only gained a new vice by my companionship with these men ; it had developed pride in me to a morbid extreme, and my self-confidence in teaching what I did not know amounted almost to insanity. When I now think over that time, and remember my own state of mind, and that of these men (a state of mind common enough among thousands still) it seems to me pitiful, terrible and ridiculous ; it excites the feelings which overcome us as we pass through a madhouse. We were all then convinced that it behooved us to speak, to write, and to print as fast as we could, as much as we could, and that on this depended the welfare of the human race. Hundreds of us wrote, printed and taught, and all the while confuted and abused each other. Quite unconscious that we ourselves knew nothing, that to the simplest of all problems in life—what is right and what is wrong—we had no answer, we all went on talking together without one to listen, at times abetting and praising one another on condition that we were abetted and praised in turn, and again turning upon each other in wrath —in short, we reproduced the scenes in a madhouse.

" Hundreds of exhausted laborers worked day

and night, putting up the type and printing millions of pages, to be spread by the post all over
Russia, and still we continued to teach, unable
to teach enough, angrily complaining the while
that we were not listened to. A strange state
of things, indeed, but now it is clear enough.
The real motive that inspired all our reasoning was the desire for money and praise, to
obtain which we knew of no other means than
writing books and newspapers. In order, however, while thus uselessly employed, to hold fast
to the conviction that we were really of importance to society, it was necessary to justify our
occupation to ourselves by another theory, and
the following was the one we adopted : ' Whatever
is, is right ; everything that is, is due to development, and the latter again to civilization ; the
measure of civilization is the figure to which the
publication of books and newspapers reaches ; we
are paid and honored for the books and newspapers which we write, and we are, therefore, the
most useful and best of all citizens.'

"'This reasoning might have been conclusive,
had we all been agreed ; but, as for every opinion
expressed by one of us there instantly appeared,
from another, one diametrically opposite, we had
to hesitate before accepting it. But this we
passed over ; we received money and were
praised by those who agreed with us, conse-
quently we were in the right. It is now clear to

me that between ourselves and the inhabitants of a madhouse there was no difference ; at the time I only vaguely suspected this, and, like all mad-men, thought all were mad except myself."

It was during this time of brilliant outward success that Count Tolstoi began to be perplexed about the value of his ideals, the meaning of life, and the uselessness of all effort in the direction of progress and perfection. He had held to the doctrine of progress or development with a sort of superstition—as the only philosophy which gave life a meaning and made effort rational. The first protest within him against this super-ficial doctrine arose on the side of feeling rather than of reason, as indicated in the following paragraph from " My Confession " :

" Thus, during my stay in Paris, the sight of a public execution revealed to me the weakness of my superstitious belief in progress. When I saw the head divided from the body, and heard the sound with which they fell separately into the box, I understood, not with my reason, but with my whole being, that no theory of the wisdom of all established things, nor of progress, could jus-tify such an act ; and that if all the men in the world, from the day of creation, by whatever theory, had found this thing necessary, it was not so ; it was a bad thing, and that, therefore, I must judge of what was right and necessary, not by what men said and did, not by progress, but what I felt to be true in my heart."

The death of his brother, after a year of painful illness, also filled him with anxious questionings which the doctrine of development could no more satisfy than the inquiry, " Where are we to steer ? " of a man drifting in a boat could be answered by saying, " We are being carried somewhere."

Partly to quiet his mental unrest by work of a more practical and beneficent kind, he devoted himself, after returning a second time from abroad, in 1861, to schemes and labors in the way of popular education, with special reference to the improvement of the serfs who had just been freed. He became a local magistrate or arbitrator, established schools for the instruction of the ignorant and edited an educational journal. But his mind was profoundly dissatisfied with his work. He felt that he was assuming the function of teacher without knowing what or how to teach, and finally, worn out by the inward struggle and intolerable contradiction, he gave up all and started for the steppes to recuperate his wasted energies.

Soon after his return, in 1862, he married, and for fifteen years the happiness of his married life, together with the new cares and occupations which it brought, served to quiet the inward turmoil from which he suffered, and his rising doubts were kept in abeyance.

" In this way," says he, " fifteen years, passed.

Notwithstanding that during these fifteen years I looked upon the craft of authorship as a very trifling thing, I still continued to write. . . . In my writings I taught what for me was the only truth, that the object of life should be our own happiness and that of our family." It was during these years that he wrote "War and Peace," and "Anna Karénina."

But such a conflict as had been awakened in him could not be long postponed or easily allayed. There was nothing new or unusual in his state of mind, but he could not rest short of some explanation or doctrine that would lend validity to existence and answer for a working theory of life. He recognized that he was mentally ill—afflicted with the measles of doubt—and he could find no peace until the evil disease should be expelled and health and soundness restored. He was in search of a faith, and could not rest until he found it. Schopenhauer's pessimism brought him no relief, for it left no logical or consistent course but suicide, and for suicide he was not prepared. So long as he was willing to live he could not without self-stultification accept the creed of the pessimist. He could not tell *why* he desired to live, unless it was in order that he might clear up his mental confusion, but he was not willing to take his own life, and kept sharp watch over himself, even to the hiding of a piece of cord, to avoid the temptation to hang himself in some moment of sudden impulse.

To give the solution of these difficulties which he finally reached and describe the faith which restored harmony to his life would be to reproduce the entire substance of his two books, "My Confession," and "My Religion"—a task which is impossible within the limits of the present volume. But that this passage in his experience is the one which most characteristically sets forth the future of the man and the phase of his work in which he penetrates farthest into the core of reality, there can be no manner of doubt.

CHAPTER VIII.

THE WRITTEN WORKS OF COUNT TOLSTOI.

THE one impression made upon the minds of these travellers in Russia, whenever they met the friends and family and admirers of Count Tolstoi, was, that it was a great pity "Leo" should abandon the congenial work of fiction for the harder school of the moralist, the reformer, and the Scriptural Exegete.

At the Winter Palace and the Marble Palace, as well as on Prince Ourouzeff's plantation, the sigh of regret was heard on all sides, "Oh, if Leo would only keep to his stories, and let his reforms alone!"

This sigh of the Russian social world over the moral waywardness of Tolstoi's genius, was everywhere most marked. Miss Isabel Hapgood, in her preface to the translations of Tolstoi's "Childhood, Boyhood and Youth," remarks, "It is to be hoped that he will return to literature, as Turgenief besought him upon his death-bed to do, and that he will, at some future day, complete these memoirs."

But the almost universal condemnation of Count Tolstoi's story, "The Kreutzer Sonata,"

shows us, most unmistakably, that the morbid
element in his mind is more baleful in the realistic realm of Zola's specialty, than in the less
attractive fields of morals, theology and political
economy.

Count Tolstoi has done his best work as a
novelist already, and, in his present mood of
mind, it were better for him to move onward up
to ethical problems, than to linger over the field
where his distorted and diseased imagination can
hold sway.

That Count Tolstoi is a man of genius and one
of the most sincere and original thinkers of his
time, no one at all acquainted with his writings
will think of questioning. Nor will close scru-
tiny of his life fail to show him also a man of
high moral qualities, and strong instincts for the
right, however they may have been repressed and
obscured by the contagious vices of the courtly
social world of Russia, which, in his earlier years,
held him, almost by force, in its embrace : and,
however one-sided and unsatisfactory his latest
speculations upon the issues of life and death
may seem to us, whatever may be its limitations
of one kind or another, Count Tolstoi's genius is
certainly of a very high order, and of an extraordinary character. And it is especially wonderful in this, that its varied manifestations give
assurance that it would have made him eminent
in whatever field, for intellectual effort, he might

have sought eminence with any persistent energy ; in any aim in which he could have had a full and continuous faith to inspire him with such persist- ence. His discussion of military affairs and tactics in many of his works, and, especially his treatment of great movements in the Russo- Napoleonic wars, show that there was in him the making of a great commander, if only, for any considerable time, he had had the ambition and opportunity to become such. It is, perhaps, evidence of a still higher genius, that he had the power of will and of conscience calmly to cast away that ambition.

Almost simultaneously with his brief but brill- iant army life, began his splendid achievements as a novelist, among which we include his grand early portraiture of man and nature in the Cauca- sus ; and no critic, except himself, in his later mor- bid mood, will think of denying the magnificence of his genius in this field. Then came his life as a philanthropist, a teacher of the most ignorant classes in schools, by himself and through others, as he had before thought to teach the educated classes through his books ; and a benefactor in every way that he could devise, of a crushed and degraded peasantry.

And here, in the execution of his plans, he often fell short of what a shrewd and practical man of mere talent, with the same aims, would have accomplished. In the infinite pity of his

great heart, for his poorer countrymen, he undoubtedly made the great mistake of believing
that the wrongs of centuries can be righted
instantly at the will of any man or set of men,
however powerful. He did not recognize that
the comfort, the prosperity, the virtues of a
class or race, are things of growth, to be cultivated patiently as well as vigorously, and not a
structure to be hastily erected upon the ruins of
one as hastily demolished. But, notwithstanding
all this, we must recognize a noble and beneficent
genius in the scope of the ideal field of effort
and sacrifice which he marked out for himself,
and all whom he could persuade to follow him, in
behalf of the class which he believed had been
long robbed and oppressed by himself, his ancestors and the class to which he and they belonged.

An ideal of conduct, which seems too lofty for
the common world of to-day, may, if held up by
the hand of genius, become the standard of every-
day thought for the next generation ; and, as in
Count Tolstoi's case, may at once begin to influence those whom it cannot absolutely control.

Finally, his observations as a philanthropist,
and his consequent study of the Scriptures, have
made Count Tolstoi the founder of a new sect, or,
as one of his admirers puts it more strongly, the
prophet of a new religion. And here, again, we
discover that it is the force of his marvellous
genius which enables him to command the re-

spectful and admiring attention of the world to teachings, most of which would be scouted if presented by a writer of merely ordinary talent.

In all the phases of his life, as a man of thought and action, Count Tolstoi is still the man of genius. If we ask what are the elements of that genius, the analysis is not difficult. In one of his later penitential confessions, he declares, regretfully, that at one period of his life he worshipped "the Ego," and at another "Force." And yet, in a certain sense, a little varying from his own definitions, "the Ego" and "Force" are the very foundations of his genius, and of all that it has accomplished. His intense personality is apparent in all his writings and all his acts, constantly and conspicuously, beyond precedent furnished by any other author. And, as we find him now in the last phase of his life—that of self-renunciation—he believes that he has entirely renounced "the worship of the 'Ego,'" while, in fact, it is more completely his master than it was when he believed that he was worshipping it, since the real object of his idolatry was the phantasm of a corrupt life, which enveloped it and concealed him from himself. Now, it is his own observations of life, his own study of the Scriptures in their original tongues, his own logic in interpreting them, that make him "the prophet of a new religion." By reading, by travel, by personal intercourse with scholars in theology, he has become familiar with all the creeds of the world, and the authorities upon which they are based, only to renounce all allegiance to any and all of them, and submit himself to the rule of "the Ego." Intellectually, he himself is now sole lord of himself.

Moreover, his personal force, his vigor of mind and body, native in a great degree, but sedulously and painfully cultivated, is a foundation-stone of his genius, without which the superstructure could not have arisen. Few of the elements which we find in that superstructure could have belonged to a mind deficient in mental or moral force, or, indeed, which was not endowed with both in a measure far beyond that of most eminent authors. That Count Tolstoi does possess this quality in that super-eminent degree is apparent to all sympathetic readers of his books. They recognize, with delight, the vigorous spirit of the mind which comes in contact with their own, and find themselves, at least for a moment and in some degree, imbued with its healthfulness ; for mental health—and, for that matter, physical health— may be as contagious as disease. If Leo Tolstoi could not rightfully be a worshipper of force, he might well thankfully worship the Power which endowed him with it, and with the will to increase and discipline it.

Not the least essential element in his genius for authorship is his surpassing faculty for observing and memorizing events, scenes and persons. No details escape him ; none are dimly seen ; none are forgotten ; and, however diverse in kind, and however numerous they may be, they never obscure or distort his view of the grand whole. This faculty, together with his admirable skill in constructing his stories, renders the result of his studies from life in that form—like paintings in which a strong grasp of outline and a bold dash in bringing out salient features are combined with an exquisite finish of minutiæ—so inwrought on the canvas that, while they do not disturb the first vivid impression they add to that which grows upon him under the continued contemplation of any true masterpiece. This is a combination rare in the painter's art, and certainly not less rare in the art of the novelist. With the doubtful exception of Dickens, we find it in no voluminous writer in such perfection as in Tolstoi. With him, as a novelist, the faculty for observing and memorizing is indispensable. His stories are mosaics, composed of bits of fact and thought—very rarely bits of fancy—so arranged and shaded into each other as to form pictures strictly after real life as he has observed it. It was needful that his mind should be plentifully supplied with material for these mosaics, and that each should be at instant command when its place in the picture was ready for it. Something of the value of such collected material to the novelist may be learned from Hawthorne's Note-books. But Hawthorne's material of this kind was carefully noted down, while Tolstoi, although he had his full note-books had, as well, a memory still more abundantly stored. Contrary to what this difference would seem to indicate, Hawthorne idealizes almost everything which he touches ; Tolstoi almost nothing. In his novels he shows little imagination beyond what is needful to arrange his material in a consecutive and effective narrative form. It is his clear, vigorous, vivacious style, with the earnest opinions and quick, deep feelings that inspire it, which gives this indefinable charm to his books. We perceive constantly that what we read is not only realistic, but, in the mind of the writer, absolutely and intensely real. The imagination exercised is no more than a good historian uses in giving truthful form and spirit to his story, while strictly conforming to the many sources of information from which it is derived. It is very near akin to that which enables a great pleader in a criminal case, bound by all the laws of evidence, to frame from the testimony of many discordant witnesses a theory satisfactory to the jury.

Tolstoi's extraordinary faculty of observation and memory must surely be accounted a very substantial element in his genius as a novelist, while that of imagination contributes very little, until we reach his latest works in a novel form.

In one of these later stories, one of his heroes is depicted as a disappointed devotee of a mystic-politico religion, which he represents as at least one form of freemasonry. Here his imagination found full, but not absolutely free, play. It is still governed by his keen and profound, if sometimes too jealous, knowledge of men. This, however, was the connecting link between Tolstoi the novelist, severely portraying real life, and Tolstoi the religious and political reformer, with all that he had learned of reality in the past and present beneath his feet, reaching upward to an ideal future only to be attained by crushing out of existence all that characterizes and rules the present, which he regards as only a superficially refined form of an evil past. In his writings upon religious, political and cognate moral themes, he gives evidence of his broad and accurate learning, and of his extended observation of facts affecting these themes ; but these are hardly more than prosaic aids in their study and exposition. It is the glorious and lofty imagination of the lover of his kind, become poet—perhaps prophet—in his ideal conception of its better future, which gives their peculiar tone to Count Tolstoi's latest writings, and raises them to the rank of works of genius.

But there is another element in Tolstoi's genius from which, more than any other, it derives its most peculiar and characteristic tone ; and this is his profound capacity for introspection, and his habit of exercising it constantly upon himself, and in the study of other minds when he finds occasion for it. In regard to himself, the impulse of self-study, self-judgment, self-revelation, seems to have been irresistible. Even in his most frivolous and dissolute early years, we find it compelling him to look into his inner life, with the result of self-condemnation which finally drove him to pursuits at least outwardly more pure. But it also furnished him with material to be interwoven into many novels and to give color to them. In each succeeding period of his life, we find this habitual self-introspection operating with ever increasing force ; always, after awhile, rendering him dissatisfied—the more proper word may be disgusted—with his present stage of advancement and painfully forcing him on to the next step. His self-judgment may often be too severe and unqualified ; his transition from one phase of thought, feeling and belief may be abnormally abrupt ; but, however violent these transitions may be, he always takes with him from one plane of life to another, not only his accumulated store of facts and learning, but also that flood of feeling whose slender fountain we see in his earliest life, and which we can watch, as, swelling in violence, it grows more and more impetuous and irresistible. To change the metaphor, the germs of his latest beliefs and governing principles appear in his earliest expressions of thought and feeling ; and we can easily watch their development and growth from seed-time to harvest. It is all apparent in his books, to which it always gives their tone, color and direction. It is often said that he is himself the hero of his own stories, and this is literally true of the earlier ones,— " The Cossacks," " Childhood, Boyhood and Youth," and several of his shorter but quite as interesting and characteristic tales.

In his later novels the conflicting moods and opinions which are agitating his own mind are divided among appropriate characters ; three at least being thus inspired in one work, " War and Peace." But, invariably, however introduced, what he sees in his inmost self is reflected with realistic vividness. His very latest works are avowedly autobiographical.

The elements which go to make up Count Tolstoi's genius are these : intense personality; healthful, masculine force in all his nature, both mental and physical ; unequalled powers of observation and memory ; an exceptionally keen and profound faculty of introspection, unflinchingly and unsparingly exercised upon himself ; extreme conscientiousness and never-failing fidelity to truth ;—these, with such modicum of imagination as is indispensable to make their fruits available for the purpose of the novelist ; and such larger proportion of that faculty in later years as carried him into regions of a higher idealism.

It is hardly necessary to say that there can be no intelligent consideration of works inspired by a genius like this, without a parallel consideration of the life of the author. It is the excess in Count Tolstoi of the qualities named, which so closely identifies him with his books, that they cannot well be treated separately. It is this, also, which gives them their admirable realism and earnestness, which constantly says to the reader, "This is no soothing amusement for a leisure hour that I offer you, but a faithful picture of the world and the evil which is in it, for you and me to remedy, as we have helped to create it. It is the social life in whose grossest vices I have participated, that I now arraign before the tribunal of society's conscience, as I have already arraigned it before my own. It is the robbery and oppression by which we of the ruling class have long crushed to earth the poor and the weak, of which I ask you to repent and aid me in redressing. In the guise of fiction, I present to you, as vividly as I can, those great truths which should inspire you with an earnest purpose to do what in you lies to serve the right and overthrow the wrong."

It is true that in none of his novels does he avow any such noble purpose, and that in his confessions he expressly disclaims any except low and selfish motives for authorship. Nevertheless, those which we have ascribed to him appear more and more clearly in each succeeding publication ; more and more governing their character, until, in the latest, they seem to have attained to absolute control. Consciously or unconsciously, he is always the teacher of righteousness, without parading it as his mission. He paints the vices of his age and nation, but even while he describes himself indulging in them— never in such form as to make them attractive. To be sure he tells the story of gambling, adultery, drunkenness and other national vices with true Russian nonchalance, rarely expressing any abhorrence of them in terms—rarely denouncing them as sins. Thus, in his great novel " Anna Karènina," where a life of illicit love ends in utter misery and suicide, he by no means characterizes this as a special judgment in punishment for a violation of the seventh commandment, but as the logical and inevitable consequence of such a life, even when led by a man and woman to whom he ascribes all noble qualities not inconsistent with it. Throughout his works, as in this, we still find him invariably teaching, as the result of his observation of life, the one old lesson of all lives, that

> " Sorrow follows wrong
> As echo follows song,
>   On, on forever."

It is a natural inquiry in regard to an author, What conditions and experiences of life gave him his opportunities for observation, and inspired him with the deep feeling which he exhibits from the first, and which has finally overmastered him ?

But great as are Count Tolstoi's novels, his religious writings show even more genius. No such book of probing, searching, moral value has appeared since St. Augustine's Confession, as Tolstoi's wonderful work, "My Confession," which, in some way, seems to put a new flooring into the worn-out moral tone of those who have pondered its meaning. And the seven discourses which follow this work and which are called " The Spirit of Christ's Teachings," reveal a depth of spiritual insight and an originality of exegesis in the study of the Bible, which remind us of the fearless common-sense of John Bunyan in his " Pilgrim's Progress," or Sir Thomas Browne in his " Religio Medici," and prepare us for that original interpretation of the Scriptures which marks the pages of his later theological work, " My Religion."

As an illustration of his original and penetrating method of interpreting familiar passages in the Word of God, let the following passages speak for themselves :

" If there are any who doubt the life beyond the grave and salvation based upon redemption, none can doubt the salvation of all men, and of each

individual man, if they will accept the evidence
of the destruction of the personal life and follow
the true way to safety by bringing their personal
wills into harmony with the will of God. Let
each man endowed with reason ask himself,
What is life? and What is death? and let him try
to give life and death another meaning than
that revealed by Jesus, and he will find that
any attempt to find in life a meaning not based
upon the renunciation of self, the service of
humanity, of the Son of man, is utterly futile.
It cannot be doubted that the personal life is condemned to destruction and that a life conforma-
ble to the will of God alone gives the possibility
of salvation. It is not much in comparison with
the sublime belief in the future life! It is not
much, but it is sure.

"I am lost with my companions in a snow-
storm. One of them assures me, with the utmost
sincerity, that he sees a light in the distance, but
it is only a mirage which deceives us both; we
strive to reach this light, but we never can find
it. Another resolutely brushes away the snow;
he seeks and finds the road, and he cries to us,
'Go not that way, the light you see is false, you
will wander to destruction; here is the road, I
felt it beneath my feet; we are saved!' It is
very little, we say. We had faith in that light
that gleamed in our deluded eyes, that told us of
a refuge, a warm shelter, rest, deliverance,—and

now, in exchange for it, we have nothing but the road. Ah, but if we continue to travel towards the imaginary light, we shall perish ; if we follow the road, we shall surely arrive at a haven of safety.

" What, then, must I do, if I, alone, understand the doctrine of Jesus, and I, alone, have trust in it among a people who neither understand it nor obey it ? What ought I to do—to live like the rest of the world, or to live according to the doctrine of Jesus ? I understood the doctrine of Jesus as expressed in his commandments, and I believed that the practice of these commandments would bring happiness to me and to all men. I understood that the fulfillment of these commandments is the will of God, the source of life. More than this, I saw that I should die like a brute after a farcical existence if I did not fulfill the will of God, and that the only chance of salvation lay in the fulfillment of his will. In following the example of the world about me I should unquestionably act contrary to the welfare of all men, and, above all, contrary to the will of the Giver of Life ; I should surely forfeit the sole possibility of bettering my desperate condition. In following the doctrine of Jesus I should continue the work common to all men who had lived before me ; I should contribute to the welfare of my fellows and of those who were to live after me ; I should obey the command of the Giver of

Life ;—I should seize upon the only hope of salvation.

"The circus at Berditchef" is in flames. A crowd of people are struggling before the only place of exit,—a door that opens inward. Suddenly, in the midst of the crowd, a voice rings out : 'Back, stand back from the door ; the closer you press against it, the less the chance of escape ; stand back ; that is your only chance of safety !'

"Whether I am alone in understanding this command or whether others with me also hear and understand, I have but one duty, and that is, from the moment I have heard and understood, to fall back from the door, and to call on everyone to obey the voice of the Saviour. I may be suffocated, I may be crushed beneath the feet of the multitude, I may perish ; my sole chance of safety is to do the one thing necessary to gain an exit. And I can do nothing else. A saviour should be a saviour, that is, one who saves. And the salvation of Jesus is the true salvation. He came, He preached His doctrine, and humanity is saved.

"The circus may burn in an hour, and those penned up in it may have no time to escape. But the world has been burning for eighteen hundred years. It has burned ever since Jesus said, '*I am come to send fire on the earth ;*' and I suffer as it burns ; and it will continue to burn until humanity is saved. Was not this fire kindled that men might have the felicity of salvation ? Understanding this, I understood and believed that Jesus is not only the Messiah—that is, the Anointed One, the Christ—but that He is in truth the Saviour of the world. I know that He is the only way ; that there is no other way for me, or for those who are tormented with me in this life. I know that for me, as for all, there is no other safety than the fulfillment of the commandments of Jesus, who gave to all humanity the greatest conceivable sum of benefits. Would there be great trials to endure ? Should I die in following the doctrine of Jesus ? This question did not alarm me. It might seem frightful to anyone who does not realize the nothingness and absurdity of an isolated personal life, and who believes that he will never die. But I know that my life, considered in relation to my individual happiness, is, taken by itself, a stupendous farce, and that this meaningless existence will end in a stupid death. Knowing this, I have nothing to fear. I shall die as all others die who do not observe the doctrine of Jesus ; but my life and my death will have a meaning for myself and for others. My life and my death will have added something to the life and salvation of others, and this will be in accordance with the doctrine of Jesus."

The following passage, or table, is, after all, a

clear insight into the very heart of all Tolstoi's religious writings :

" There is no man that hath left house, or brethren, or sisters, or mother, or father, or children, or lands, for my sake and for the Gospel's sake, but he shall receive a hundredfold now in this time, houses, and brethren, and sisters, and mothers, and children, and lands with persecutions, and, in the age to come, eternal life." (Mark 10 : 28–30.)

" Jesus declared it is true that those who follow His doctrine must expect to be persecuted by those who do not follow it ; but He did not say that His disciples will be the worse off for that reason. On the contrary, He said that His disciples would have, here in this world, more benefits than those who did not follow Him. That Jesus said and thought this is beyond a doubt, as the clearness of His words on this subject, the meaning of His entire doctrine, His life and the life of His disciples, plainly show. But was His teaching in this respect true ?

" When we examine the question as to which of the two conditions would be the better, that of the disciples of Jesus or that of the disciples of the world, we are obliged to conclude that the condition of the disciples of Jesus ought to be the most desirable, since the disciples of Jesus, in doing good to everyone, would not arouse the hatred of men. The disciples of Jesus, doing evil to no one, would be persecuted only by the wicked. The disciples of the world, on the contrary, are likely to be persecuted by everyone, since the law of the disciples of the world is the law of each for himself—the law of struggle, that is, of mutual persecution. Moreover, the disciples of Jesus would be prepared for suffering, while the disciples of the world use all possible means to avoid suffering. The disciples of Jesus would feel that their sufferings were useful to the world ; but the disciples of the world do not know why they suffer. On abstract grounds, then, the condition of disciples of Jesus would be more advantageous than that of the disciples of the world. But is it so in reality ? To answer this, let each one call to mind all the painful moments of his life, all the physical and moral sufferings that he has endured; and let him ask himself if he has suffered these calamities in behalf of the doctrine of the world or in behalf of the doctrine of Jesus. Every sincere man will find, in recalling his past life, that he has never once suffered for practising the doctrine of Jesus. He will find that the greater part of the misfortunes of his life have resulted from following the doctrines of the world. In my own life (an exceptionally happy one from a worldly point of view) I can reckon up as much suffering caused by following the doctrine of the world as many a martyr has endured for the doctrine of Jesus. All the most painful moments of my life, the orgies and duels in which I took part

as a student, the wars in which I have participated, the diseases I have endured, and the
abnormal and insupportable conditions under
which I now live, all these are only so much
martyrdom exacted by fidelity to the doctrine of
the world. But I speak of a life exceptionally
happy from a worldly point of view. How many
martyrs have suffered for the doctrine of the
world torments that I should find difficulty in
enumerating!

"We do not realize the difficulties and dangers
entailed by the practice of the doctrine of the
world, simply because we are persuaded that we
could not do otherwise than follow that doctrine.
We are persuaded that all the calamities that we
inflict upon ourselves are the result of the inevitable conditions of life, and we cannot understand
that the doctrine of Jesus teaches us how we may
rid ourselves of these calamities and render our
lives happy. To be able to reply to the question,
Which of these two conditions is the happier? we
must, at least for the time being, put aside our
prejudices, and take a careful survey of our surroundings. Go through our great cities and
observe the emancipated, sickly, and distorted
specimens of humanity to be found therein; recall
your own existence and that of the people with
whose lives you are familiar; recall the instances
of violent deaths and suicides of which you have
heard,—and ask yourself for what cause all this

suffering and death, this despair that leads to suicide, has been endured. You will find, perhaps to your surprise, that nine-tenths of all human suffering endured by men is useless, and ought not to exist, that, in fact, the majority of men are martyrs to the doctrine of the world.

"One rainy autumn day I rode on the tramway by the Sukhareff Tower in Moscow. For the distance of half a verst the vehicle forced its way through a compact crowd which quickly reformed its ranks. From morning till night these thousands of men—the greater portion of them starving and in rags—tramped angrily through the mud, venting their hatred in abusive epithets and acts of violence. The same sight may be seen in all the market-places of Moscow. At sunset these people go to the taverns and gaming-houses; their nights are passed in filth and wretchedness. Think of the lives of these people, of what they abandon through choice for their present condition; think of the heavy burden of labor without reward which weighs upon these men and women, and you will see that they are true martyrs. All these people have forsaken houses, lands, parents, wives, children; they have renounced all the comforts of life, and they have come to the cities to acquire that which according to the gospel of the world is indispensable to every one. And all these tens of thousands of unhappy people sleep in hovels, and subsist upon strong drink and wretched food. But, aside from this class—all, from factory workman, cab-driver, sewing girl, and lorette, to merchant and government official—all endure the most painful and abnormal conditions without being able to acquire what, according to the doctrine of the world, is indispensable to each."

CHAPTER IX.

THE WRITTEN WORKS OF COUNT TOLSTOI.
(*Continued.*)

" SEEK among all these men, from beggar to millionaire, one who is contented with his lot, and you will not find one such in a thousand. Each one spends his strength in pursuit of what is exacted by the doctrine of the world, and of what he is unhappy not to possess ; and scarcely has he obtained one object of his desires when he strives for another, and still another, in that infinite labor of Sisyphus which destroys the lives of men. Run over the scale of individual fortunes, ranging from a yearly income of 300 roubles to 50,000 roubles, and you will rarely find a person who is not striving to gain 400 roubles if he have 300 ; 500 if he have 400, and so on to the top of the ladder. Among them all you will rarely find one who, with 500 roubles, is willing to adopt the mode of life of him who has only 400. When such an instance does occur, it is not inspired by a desire to make life more simple, but to amass money and make it more sure. Each strives, continually, to make the heavy burden of existence still more heavy, by giving himself up, body and soul, to the practice of the doctrine of the world.

To-day we must buy an overcoat and galoches, to-morrow a watch and chain ; the next day we must install ourselves in an apartment with a sofa and a bronze lamp ; then we must have carpets and velvet gowns, horses and carriages, paintings and decorations, and then—then we fall ill of overwork and die. Another continues the same task, sacrifices his life to the same Moloch, and then dies also without realizing for what he has lived. But, possibly, this existence is in itself attractive ? Compare it with what men have always called happiness, and you will see that it is hideous. For what, according to the general estimate, are the principal conditions of earthly happiness ?

" I. One of the first conditions of happiness is that the link between man and nature shall not be severed—that is, that he shall be able to see the sky above him, and that he shall be able to enjoy the sunshine, the pure air, the fields with their verdure, their multitudinous life. Men have always regarded it as a great unhappiness to be deprived of all these things, but what is the condition of those men who live according to the doctrine of the world ? The greater their success in practising the doctrine of the world, the more they are deprived of these conditions of happiness. The greater their worldly success, the less they are able to enjoy the light of the sun, the freshness of the fields and woods, and all the delights of country life. Many of them—including nearly all

the women—arrive at old age without having seen
the sun rise, or the beauties of the early morning ;
without having seen a forest, except from a seat
in a carriage ; without ever having planted a
field or a garden, and without having the least
idea as to the ways and habits of dumb animals.
These people, surrounded by artificial light,
instead of sunshine, look only upon fabrics of
tapestry, and stone, and wood, fashioned by the
hand of man. The roar of machinery, the roll of
vehicles, the thunder of cannon, the sound of musical instruments are always in their ears ; they
breathe an atmosphere heavy with distilled per-
fumes and tobacco smoke. Because of the weakness of their stomachs, and their depraved tastes,
they eat rich and highly spiced food. When they
move about from place to place, they travel in
closed carriages ; when they go into the country
they have the same fabrics beneath their feet ;
the same draperies shut out the sunshine ; and
the same array of servants cut off all communi-
cation with the men, the earth, the vegetation,
and the animals about them. Wherever they go,
they are like so many captives shut out from the
conditions of happiness. As prisoners sometimes
console themselves with a blade of grass that
forces its way through the pavement of their
prison-yard, or make pets of a spider or a mouse,
so these people sometimes amuse themselves with
sickly plants, a parrot, a poodle, or a monkey, to

whose needs, however, they do not themselves administer.

"II. Another inevitable condition of happiness is WORK : first, intellectual labor that one is free to choose and love ; secondly, the exercise of physical power that brings a good appetite, and tranquil and profound sleep.

"Here, again, the greater the imagined prosperity that falls to the lot of men, according to the doctrine of the world, the more such men are deprived of this condition of happiness. All the prosperous people of the world—the men of dignity and wealth—are as completely deprived of the advantages of work as if they were shut up in solitary confinement. They struggle unsuccessfully with the diseases caused by the need of physical exercise, and with the *ennui* which pursues them—unsuccessfully, because labor is a pleasure only when it is necessary—and they have need of nothing ; or, they undertake work that is odious to them, like the bankers, solicitors, administrators, and government officials ; and their wives, who plan receptions and routs, and devise toilettes for themselves and their children. (I say odious, because I never yet met any person of this class who was contented with his work or took as much satisfaction in it as the porter feels in shoveling away the snow from before their doorsteps.) All these favorites of fortune are either deprived of work or are obliged to work at what they do not like, after the manner of criminals condemned to hard labor.

" III. The third undoubted condition of happiness is the *family*. But the more men are enslaved by worldly success, the more certainly are they cut off from domestic pleasures. The majority of them are libertines, who deliberately renounce the joys of family life and retain only its cares. If they are not libertines, their children, instead of being a source of pleasure, are a burden, and all possible means are employed to render marriage unfruitful. If they have children, they make no effort to cultivate the pleasures of companionship with them. They leave their children almost continually to the care of strangers, confiding them first to the instruction of persons who are usually foreigners, and then sending them to public educational institutions, so that of family life they have only the sorrows, and their children from infancy are as unhappy as their parents, and wish their parents dead, that they may become the heirs. These people are not confined in prisons, but the consequences of their way of living, with regard to the family, are more melancholy than the deprivation from domestic relations inflicted upon those who are kept in confinement under sentence of the law.

" IV. The fourth condition of happiness is sympathetic and unrestricted intercourse with all classes of men. And the higher a man is placed in the social scale, the more certainly is he deprived of this essential condition of happiness. The higher he goes, the narrower becomes his circle of associates; the lower sinks the moral and intellectual level of those to whose companionship he is restrained.

"The peasant and his wife are free to enter into friendly relations with everyone, and if a million men will have nothing to do with them, there remain eighty millions of people with whom they may fraternize—from Archangel to Astrakhan—without waiting for a ceremonious visit or an introduction. A clerk and his wife will find hundreds of people who are their equals; but the clerk of a higher rank will not admit them to a footing of social equality ; and they, in their turn, are excluded by others. The wealthy man of the world reckons by dozens the families with whom he is willing to maintain social ties—all the rest of the world are strangers. For the cabinet-minister and the millionaire, there are only a dozen people as rich and as important as themselves. For kings and emperors the circle is still more narrow. Is not the whole system like a great prison where each inmate is restricted to association with a few fellow-convicts ?

"V. Finally, the fifth condition of happiness is _bodily health_. And once more we find, that as we ascend the social scale, this condition of happiness is less and less within the reach of the

followers of the doctrine of the world. Compare
a family of medium social status with a family of
peasants. The latter toil unremittingly and are
robust of body; the former is made up of men and
women more or less subject to disease. Recall
to mind the rich men and women you have known
—are not most of them invalids ? A person of
that class whose physical disabilities do not
oblige him to take a periodical course of hygienic
and medical treatment, is as rare as an invalid
among the laboring classes. All these favorites
of fortune are the victims and practitioners of
sexual vices that have become a second nature,
and they are toothless, gray, and bald, at an age
when a workingman is in the prime of manhood.
Nearly all are afflicted with nervous or other
diseases arising from excesses in eating, drunkenness, luxury, and perpetual medication. Those
who do not die young, pass half their lives under
the influence of morphine or other drugs, as melancholy wrecks of humanity, incapable of self-
attention ; leading a parasitic existence like that
of a certain species of ants which are nourished
by their slaves. Here is the death list : One has
blown out his brains ; another has rotted away
from the effects of syphilitic poison ; this old man
succumbed to sexual excess; this young man to
a wild outburst of sensuality ; one died of drunkenness, another of gluttony, another from the
abuse of morphine, another from an induced

abortion. One after another they perished—
victims of the *doctrine of the world*. And a multitude presses on behind them, like an army of
martyrs, to undergo the same sufferings, the same
perdition.

"*To follow the doctrine of Jesus is difficult!*
Jesus said that they who would forsake houses,
and lands, and brethren, and follow His doctrine,
should receive a hundredfold in houses, and lands,
and brethren ; and besides all this, eternal life.
And no one is willing even to make the experiment. The doctrine of the world commands its
followers to leave houses, and lands, and brethren;
to forsake the country for the filth of the city,
there to toil as a bath-keeper, soaping the backs
of others; as an apprentice in a little underground
shop, passing life in counting copecks; as a prosecuting attorney, to serve in bringing unhappy
wretches under condemnation of the law ; as a
cabinet-minister, perpetually signing documents
of no importance ; as the head of an army, killing
men. 'Forsake all and live this hideous life ending in a cruel death, and you shall receive nothing
in this world or the other,' is the command ; and
everyone listens and obeys. Jesus tells us to take
up the cross and follow Him, to bear submissively
the lot apportioned out to us. No one hears His
words or follows His command. But let a man in
a uniform decked out with gold lace, a man whose
specialty is to kill his fellows, say, 'Take, not

your cross, but your knapsack and carbine and march to suffering and certain death,' and a mighty host is ready to receive his orders. Leaving parents, wives, and children; clad in grotesque costumes ; subject to the will of the first comer of a higher rank ; famished, benumbed and exhausted by forced marches they go, like a herd of cattle to the slaughter-house, not knowing where, —and yet these are not cattle, they are men. With despair in their hearts they move on to die of hunger, or cold, or disease, or, if they survive, to be brought within range of a storm of bullets and commanded to kill. They kill and are killed, no one knows why or to what end. An ambitious stripling has only to brandish his sword and shout a few magniloquent words to induce them to rush to certain death. And yet no one finds this to be difficult. Neither the victims nor those whom they have forsaken find anything difficult in such sacrifices, in which parents encourage their children to take part. It seems to them not only that such should be, but that they could not be otherwise, and that they are altogether admirable and moral."

Surely nothing stronger than this has been written in this century. It is stronger than anything Carlyle or Ruskin have penned, simply because the life has been back of the writing to underscore it and make it emphatic.

The best known of Count Tolstoi's works are

as follows : "Anna Karénina," "Childhood, Boyhood, Youth," "What to Do," "Ivan Ilyitch,"
"Family Happiness," "My Confession," "My
Religion," "Life," "Napoleon's Russian Campaign," "Power and Liberty," "The Long Exile,"
"The Invaders," "A Russian Proprietor," "Se-
bastopol," "The Cossacks," "War and Peace."

The Tolstoi booklets, already published, are :
"Where Love Is," "The Two Pilgrims," "What
Men Live By "; and these are each little gems,
full of the fragrance and sweetness of Hans
Christian Andersen.

Tolstoi's "Boyhood, Childhood and Youth"
is one of the most attractive and fascinating bits
of autobiography ever published, and makes us
understand how the diary of Marie Bashkirtseff
came to be written, the former being the memoir
of a Russian reformer and the latter the memoir
of a Russian artist.

The glimpses we get of the boy's life at his
country home and in the city of Moscow help to
give us a clue to the true meaning of the man's
after-life, and show us, most unmistakably, his remarkable insight into the social life of the Slavic
people and his marked preparation to be a leader
and reformer among them.

His book entitled, "What to Do, or Thoughts
Evoked by the Census of Moscow," is the most
radical and logical of all his writings, and shows
us his peculiar principles of social reform applied

with the remorseless rigor of John the Baptist in the wilderness of the politico-economical world of the Russia of to-day. Let the following extracts serve as an illustration of his writing as an economist :

"I recollect once, while walking in a street in Moscow, I saw a man come out and examine the flagstones attentively ; then, choosing one of them, he sat down by it and began to scrape and rub it vigorously.

"What is he doing with the pavement ? I wondered ; and having come up close to him I discovered he was a young man from a butcher's shop, and he was sharpening his knife on the flagstone. He was not thinking about the stones when examining them, and still less while doing his work ; he was merely sharpening his knife. It was necessary for him to do so in order to cut the meat, but to me it seemed that he was doing something to the pavement.

"In the same way mankind seems to be occupied with commerce, treaties, wars, sciences, arts ; and yet for them one thing only is important, and they only do that ; they are elucidating those moral laws by which they live.

"Moral laws are already in existence, and mankind has been merely re-discovering them : this elucidation appears to be unimportant and imperceptible to one who has no need of moral law, and one who does not desire to live by it. Yet this is not only the chief, but ought to be the sole, business of all men. This elucidation is imperceptible in the same way as the difference between a sharp knife and a blunt one is imperceptible. A knife remains a knife, and one who has not got to cut anything with it will not notice its edge ; but for one who understands that all his life depends on whether his knife is blunt or sharp, every improvement in sharpening it is important ; and such a man knows that there must be no limit to this improvement, and that the knife is only really a knife when it is sharp, and when it cuts what it has to cut.

"The conviction of this truth flashed upon me when I began to write my pamphlet. Previously it seemed to me that I knew everything about my subjèct—-that I had a thorough understanding of everything connected with those questions which had been awakened in me by the impressions made in Liapin's house during the census ; but when I tried to sum them up and put them on paper, it turned out that the knife would not cut, and had to be sharpened ; so it is only now after three years that I feel my knife is sharp enough for me to cut out what I want.

"It is not that I have learned new things : my thoughts are still the same, but they were blunt formerly ; they kept scattering in every direction ; there was no edge to them ; nor was anything brought, as it is now, to the one central point, to one most simple and plain conclusion.

"I recollect that during the whole time of my unsuccessful endeavors to help the unfortunate inhabitants of Moscow, I felt that I was like a man trying to help others out of a morass, who was himself all the time stuck fast in it. Every effort made me feel the instability of the ground upon which I was standing. I was conscious that I myself was in this same morass; but this acknowledgment did not help me to look more closely under my feet, in order to ascertain the nature of the ground upon which I stood; I kept looking for some exterior means to remedy the existing evil.

"I felt that my life was a bad one, and that people ought not to live so; yet I did not come to the most natural and obvious conclusion, that I must first reform my own mode of life before I should have any conception of how to reform that of others. And so I began as it were at the wrong end. I was living in town and I desired to improve the lives of the men there; but I was soon convinced that I had no power to do so, and I began to ponder over the nature of town life and town misery. I said to myself, over and over, 'What is this town life and town misery? and Why, while living in town am I unable to help the town poor?'

"The only reply I found was that I was powerless to do anything for them : first, because there were too many collected together in one place ; secondly, because none of them was at all like those in the country. And again I asked myself, 'Why are there so many here, and in what do they differ from the country poor?' To both of these questions the answer was one and the same. There are many poor people in towns because there, all those who have nothing to subsist on in the country are collected round the rich, and their peculiarity consists only in that they have all come into the towns from the country in order to get a living. (If there are any town poor born there whose fathers and grandfathers were town-born, these in their turn originally came there to get a living.) But what are we to understand by the expression getting a living in town ? There is something strange in the expression : it sounds like a joke when we reflect on its meaning. How is it that from the country, *i. e.*, from places where there are woods, meadows, corn and cattle, where the earth yields the treasures of fertility—men come away in order to get a living in a place where there are none of these advantages but only stones and dust? What then do these words signify, to get a living in town ?

"Such a phrase is constantly used both by the employed and their employers, and that as if it were quite clear and intelligible. I remember

now all the hundreds and thousands of town people, well or in want, with whom I have spoken
about their object in coming here, and all of
them, without exception, told me they had quitted
their villages in order to get a living; that according to the proverb, 'Moscow neither sows nor
reaps yet lives in wealth'; that in Moscow there
is abundance of everything; and that therefore
in Moscow one may get the money which is
needed in the country for getting corn, cottages,
horses and other essentials of life.

"But, in fact, the source of all wealth is the
country; there only are real riches,—corn, woods,
horses and everything necessary. Why, then go
to towns in order to get what is to be had in the
country? And why should people carry away
from the country into the towns such things as
are necessary for country people,—flour, oats,
horses and cattle? Hundreds of times have I
spoken thus with peasants who live in towns;
and from my talks with them, and from my own
observations, it became clear to me that the
accumulation of country people in the cities is
partly necessary, because they could not otherwise earn their livelihood, and partly voluntary,
because they are attracted by the temptations of
a town life. It is true that the circumstances of
a peasant are such that in order to satisfy the
pecuniary demands made upon him in his village,
he cannot do it otherwise than by selling that

corn and cattle which he very well knows will be necessary for himself; and he is compelled whether he will or not, to go to town in order to earn back that which was his own. But it is also true that he is attracted to town by the charms of a comparatively easy way of getting money, and by the luxury of life there; and under the pretext of earning his living he goes there in order to have easier work and better eating, to drink tea three times a day, to dress himself smartly, and even to get drunk and lead a dissolute life.

"The cause is a simple one, for property passing from the hands of the agriculturalist into those of non-agriculturalists, thus accumulates in towns. Observe towards autumn how much wealth is gathered together in villages. Then comes the demands of taxes, rents, recruiting; then the temptations of vodka, marriages, feasts, peddlers and all sorts of other snares; so that, in one way or other, this property in all its various forms (sheep, calves, cows, horses, pigs, poultry, eggs, butter, hemp, flax, rye, oats, buckwheat, peas, hemp-seed and flax-seed) passes into the hands of strangers, and is taken first to provincial towns and from there to the capitals. A villager is compelled to dispose of all these in order to satisfy the demands made upon him, and the temptations offered him—and having thus dispensed his goods, he is left in want and must follow where his wealth has been taken; and there he tries to earn back the money necessary for his most urgent needs at home ; and so being partly carried away by these temptations he himself along with others, makes use of the accumulated wealth.

".Everywhere throughout Russia, and I think not only in Russia but all over the world, the same thing happens. The wealth of country producers passes into the hands of trades-people, land-owners, government officials, manufacturers : the men who receive this wealth want to enjoy it, and to enjoy it fully, they must be in town. In the village in the first place, owing to the inhabitants being scattered, it is difficult for the rich to gratify all their desires : you do not find there all sorts of shops, banks, restaurants, theatres and various kinds of public amusements.

" Secondly, another of the chief pleasures procured by wealth,—vanity, the desire to astonish, to make a display before others,—cannot be gratified in the country for the same reason, its inhabitants being too scattered. There is no one in the country to appreciate luxury ; there is no one to astonish. There, you may have what you like to embellish your dwelling, pictures, bronze statues, all sorts of carriages, fine toilets, but there is no one to look at them or to envy you ; the peasants do not understand the value of all this, and cannot make head nor tail of it.

" Thirdly, the luxury in the country is even

disagreeable to a man who has a conscience, and is an anxiety to a timid person. One feels uneasy or ashamed at taking a milk bath, or in feeding puppies with milk, when there are children close by needing food ; one feels the same in building pavilions and gardens among a people who live in cottages covered with stable litter, and who have no wood to burn. There is no one in the village to prevent the stupid, uneducated peasants from spoiling our comfort.

" And, therefore, rich people gather together in towns and settle near those who, in similar positions have similar desires. In towns the enjoyments of all sorts of luxuries is carefully protected by a numerous police. The chief inhabitants of the town are government functionaries, round whom all sorts of master workmen, artisans, and all the rich people have settled.

" There a rich man has only to think about anything in order to get it. It is also more agreeable for him to live there because he can gratify his vanity ; there are people with whom he may try to compete in luxury, whom he may astonish or eclipse. But it is especially pleasant for a wealthy man to live in town, because, where his country life was uncomfortable and somewhat incongruous on account of his luxury ; in town, on the contrary, it would be uncomfortable for him not to live splendidly and as his equals in wealth do.

"Money ! what then is money ? It is answered, money represents labor. I meet educated people who even assert that money represents labor performed by those who possess it. I confess that I, myself, formerly shared this opinion, although I did not very clearly understand it. But now it became necessary for me to learn thoroughly what money was.

"In order to do so I addressed myself to science. Science says that money in itself is neither unjust nor pernicious ; that money is the natural result of the conditions of social life, and is indispensable, first, for convenience of exchange; secondly, as a measure of value ; thirdly, for saving ; and fourthly, for payments.

"The evident fact that when I have in my pocket three rubles to spare, which I am not in need of, I have only to whistle and in every civilized town I obtain a hundred people ready for these three rubles, to do the worst, most disgusting and humiliating act I require ; and this comes, not from money, but from the very complicated conditions of the economical life of nations.

"The dominion of one man over others comes not from money, but from the circumstance that a workingman does not receive the full value of his labor ; and the fact that he does not get the full value of his labor, depends upon the nature of capital, rent and wages ; and upon complicated connections between them and production itself ;

and between the distribution and consumption of wealth. In plain language, it means that those who have money, may twist around their finger those who have none. But science says this is an illusion ; that in every kind of production three factors take part—land, savings of labor (capital) and labor ; and that the dominion of the few over the many, proceeds from the various connections between these factors of production, and because the first two factors, land and capital, are not in the hands of working people. From this fact, and from the various conditions resulting therefrom, proceeds this domination.

"Whence comes this great power of money, which strikes us all with a sense of its injustice and cruelty ? Why is one man by the means of money to have dominion over others ? Science says ' It comes from the division of the agents of production, and from the consequent complicated combination which oppress the workingman.'

"This answer has always appeared to me to be strange, not only because it leaves one part of the question unnoticed ; namely, the signification of money, but also because of the division of the factors of production, which to an uninformed man will always appear artificial and not in accordance with reality. It is asserted that in every production, three agents come into operation— land, capital and labor ; and along with this division, it is understood that property (or its value in money) is divided among those who possess one of these agents. Thus, rent—the value of the ground—belongs to the land-owner ; interest to the capitalist, and labor to the workingman."

"Is it really so? First, is it true that in every production three agencies operate? Now while I am writing this, around me proceeds the production of hay. Of what is this production composed? I am told of the land which produces the grass, of capital, scythes, rakes, pitch-forks, carts, which are necessary to the housing of the hay, and of labor. But I see that this is not true. Besides the land, there is the sun and rain ; besides social order which has been keeping these meadows from damage, caused by letting stray cattle graze upon them, the prudence of workingmen, their knowledge of language, and many other agencies of production, which, for some unknown reason, are not taken into consideration by political economy.

"The power of the sun is as necessary as the land. I may instance the position of men in which (as, for instance, in a town) some of them assume the right to keep out the sun from others by means of walls or trees. Why, then, is this sun not included in the agents of production?

"Rain is another means as necessary as the ground itself. The air, too, I can picture to myself men without water and pure air, because other men assume to themselves the right to monopolize these, which are essentially necessary

to all. Public security is likewise a necessary
. element ; food and dress in workmen are similar
means in production ; this last is even recognized
by some economists. Education, the knowledge
of language which creates the possibility of reason-
able work, is likewise an agent. I could fill a
volume by enumerating such conditions unnoticed
by science. Why, then, are three only to be
chosen and laid as a foundation for the science of
political economy ? Why are the rays of the sun,
rain, food, knowledge, not equally recognized ?
Why only the land ? the instruments of labor and
the labor itself? Simply because the right of
men to enjoy the rays of the sun, rain, food, speech
and audience are challenged only on rare occasions ; but the use of land, and of the instruments
of labor are constantly challenged in society.

"This is the true foundation for it ; and the
division of these agents for production into three,
is quite arbitrary and is not involved in the
nature of things. But it may be, perhaps, urged
that this division is so suitable to man, that
wherever economical relationships form themselves, there these appear at once and alone."

Of Anna Karénina, the best criticism is that of
our own novelist, W. D. Howells, whose pure
and beautiful story, " A Hazard of New Fortunes," is the nearest approach we have yet had
to the long-expected American novel, if, in fact,
it is not the novel itself. It takes a soul to find

a soul ; it is only a poet who can rightly interpret a poet, and the judgment of one true novelist upon another, is worth our careful consideration.

"As you read on you say not, ' This is like life,' but, ' This is life.' It has not only the complexion, the very hue of life, but its movement, its advances, its strange pauses, its seeming reversion to former conditions, and its perpetual change, its apparent isolations, its essential solidarity. It is a world and you live in it while you read and long afterward ; but, at no step have you been betrayed, not because your guide has warned or exhorted you, but, because he has been true, and has shown you all things as they are."

Tolstoi's " War and Peace " is, perhaps, the best known and most read of all his stories, and leaves upon the mind the most vivid impression of the awful horror of war.

And now, after his moral and religious writings, after thrilling us with the radical simplicity of " My Confession," and " My Religion," we find Count Tolstoi returning in his dreadful " Kreutzer Sonata " to the " filth of Zola and the atmosphere of Paris and a moral morgue."

That it is a great mistake on his part, we must all admit. It does not do to defend our heroes when our heroes falter. But, at least, this much must be said, that the motive of the story was, undoubtedly, to work a reform in the abuse of the social glamour thrown around the modern marriage market, and not wilfully to revel in the filth of such a subject.

Tolstoi is a Russian with French modes of expression, and radical and fanatical views of the social life of to-day ; and the sound coming from the story has the discordant note of a barbaric Chinese gong struck by a madman—but then, everything depends upon the way one strikes a gong !

THE MARBLE PALACE.—ST. PETERSBURG.

CHAPTER X.

THE farm or plantation of Count Tolstoi's friend was a typical Russian farm-house, with hay-mows, thatched hamlets, muddy roads, thick bushes, and shortened trees as the environment of the master's house.

A brick church and chapel, or school-house, built of plain burnt red brick, with the usual Muscovitish tower and belfry, indicated the pious zeal of this stalwart lay member of the Greek Church, who was as loyal to his faith as we found our friend Lieutenant-General Kireff had been. He, too, had been to the Bönn Conference upon Christian Unity, and had met the late Bishop Young of Florida, who had also been a delegate from America.

Prince Ourouzeff conducted his guests through his library, showing them his most valuable books, his Hebrew Scriptures and manuscripts, keeping up a pleasant talk in broken English, which Count Tolstoi amplified in French and German, adding shades of expression with a pleasant run of banter as to the exact meaning of what was intended.

"Ah," said Prince Ourouzeff, when Count

Tolstoi had taken the other two to a distant corner of the library to inspect some valuable work
there, "Ah! if Leo would only keep to his novels
and let his reforms alone, how much better it
would be"; a sentiment to which the Count
subsequently replied as follows : " Dear Ourouzeff,
he is so good and so pious ! "

While showing us his Hebrew volumes, Count
Tolstoi whispered, " You do not know how pious
Ourouzeff is ! He gets up every morning at three
o'clock to read the prophets in Hebrew and the
Epistles in Greek "—a custom which our dear old
host seemed to think must be a common one with
the American clergy.

While looking over the books we came across a
copy of Derzhavin's works—a Russian poet, who
lived 1763-1816, and who was a soldier of nineteen on guard at the Winter Palace, when Catha-
rine ascended the throne.

" I think I can quote you several stanzas in
English of Derzhavin's Hymn on God " said one
of the party, " my mother taught it to me when a
boy." Thereupon the memory lasted long enough
to repeat the following verses from Sir John
Bowring's translation to these listening Russians:

> O Thou eternal One! whose presence bright
> All space doth occupy, all motion guide,
> Unchang'd through time's all-devastating flight;
> Thou only God! there is no God beside!

Being above all beings! Mighty One!
Whom none can comprehend and none explore;
Who fill'st existence with Thyself alone:
Embracing all,—supporting,—ruling o'er,—
Being whom we call God—and know no more!

In its sublime research, philosophy
May measure out the ocean deep—may count
The sands or the sun's rays—but God! for Thee
There is no weight nor measure:—none can mount
Up to Thy mysteries; reason's brightest spark,
Though kindled by Thy light, in vain would try
To trace Thy counsels, infinite and dark;
And thought is lost ere thought can soar so high,
Even like past moments in eternity.

A million torches lighted by Thy hand
Wander unwearied through the blue abyss:
They own Thy power, accomplish Thy command:
All gay with life, all eloquent with bliss,
What shall we call them! Piles of crystal light—
A glorious company of golden streams—
Lamps of celestial ether, burning bright—
Suns lighting systems with their joyous beams?
But Thou to these art as the moon to night.

Yes! as a drop of water in the sea,
All this magnificence in Thee is lost;—
What are ten thousand worlds compared to Thee?
And what am *I*, then? Heaven's unnumber'd host,
Though multiplied by myriads, and array'd
In all the glory of sublimest thought,
Is but an atom in the balance weighed,
Against Thy greatness is a cipher brought
Against infinity! What am I then?—Naught!

Naught! But the effluence of Thy light divine,
Pervading worlds, hath reached my bosom too;

Yes! in my spirit doth Thy spirit shine,
As shines the sunbeam in a drop of dew.
Naught! but I live and on Hope's pinions fly
Eager towards Thy presence; for in Thee
I live, and breathe, and dwell; aspiring high,
Even to the throne of Thy divinity.
I am, O God! and surely *Thou* must be!

Thou art! directing, guiding all.—Thou art!
Direct my understanding then to Thee;
Control my spirit, guide my wandering heart:
Though but an atom 'midst immensity,
Still I am something, fashioned by Thy hand!
I hold a middle rank 'twixt heaven and earth,
On the last verge of mortal being stand,
Close to the realms where angels have their birth,
Just on the boundaries of the spirit-land!

The chain of being is complete in me;
In me is matter's last gradation lost,
And the next step is spirit—deity!
I can command the lightning, and am dust!
A monarch, and a slave! a worm, a god!
Whence came I here, and how? so marvellously
Constructed and conceiv'd! unknown? this clod
Lives surely through some higher energy?
For from itself alone it could not be!

These verses seemed to make a deep impression upon the two Russians, and they spoke in their own tongue some words of appreciation of the English measure of verse.

The naïve simplicity of our host was well illustrated by the following conversation: " My friend," said Prince Ourouzeff, " ze standing army of ze United State is only twenty-five thousand troop ! Is zere not ze greatest danger that with only twenty-five thousand troop ze United State will be invaded by the Empire of Brazil ? " When all fear of this impending danger was removed the Prince resumed : " But with only twenty-five thousand troop in ze United State is there not great danger that ze President Harrison will seize ze rein of government and become Dictator like Boulanger ? "

Again the fears of our pious friend were put to rest, and he took Lord Byron and Mr. Thackeray into another portion of the house, and Count Tolstoi and the writer were left together to take a walk about the plantation.

In thinking in advance of this interview with Tolstoi, the following apparently original and spontaneous questions had been committed to memory :

April 11th—Interview with Tolstoi.

1. What hope is there for social reform among the Russian nobles?

2. How many are there like-minded with Count Tolstoi ?

3. What hope is there for progress in the Greek Church ?

4. Do the monks exert a good influence ?

5. Would not an order of preachers among the Greek Church do a great deal of good ?

6. What is the next step of reform in Russia ?

7. Is Nihilism on the wane?

8. Is the existing government likely to take any steps towards constitutional ruling?

9. Are the teachings of Henry George prohibited in Russia?

But not one of these questions was asked, for the Count led the way by asking all sorts of questions about America, and it seemed easier and wiser to follow his train of thought than to insert abrupt and independent questions which might not be familiar to him.

His daughter had asked us to take to him a large bundle of mail in the shape of letters and papers, and as we deposited them in his room, my eye fell on two American newspapers, the Boston *Index* and a Shaker paper from Oregon, on the Pacific coast.

On the journey to St. Petersburg, Stead's very interesting book "Truth About Russia," had been very carefully read, and the interview at Yasnaia Poliana had been most particularly studied. The very questions which were upon our minds had been asked by his English visitor and had been answered by the Russian novelist, and since these replies of Count Tolstoi are so interestingly told, the story shall be given in Mr. Stead's own words:

"Of our religious sects he was naturally most attracted by the Quakers. He had the autobiography of George Fox on his book-shelf, but he

had not yet read it. He heartily approved of the
simplicity of the Society of Friends, of the
modesty of their attire, and their use of " thee "
and " thou." He was, of course, entirely in ac-
cord with their principle of non-resistance. Only
in one thing the Friends came short of the Tol-
stoian ideal : they recognized the right of
property.

"Count Tolstoi was reluctant to speak of con-
troversial questions. He said, ' Christ in His
last prayer prayed that all His followers might be
one ; hence, I always endeavor to discover on
what points I can agree with any who follow
Christ.' It was this craving after the true Cath-
olicity—the essential unity of the Christian
Brotherhood—that led him to welcome so heartily
a little preface I had written some years ago to
' Centres of Spiritual Activity,' in which I said
that ' the Ideal Christian Church at the present
time ought to include many professing atheists
among its members, for men's definitions of themselves are not free from blunder and self-decep-
tion, and many professing atheists are unconscious
Christians.'

"Always endeavor to find out points of agree-
ment rather than those of antagonism ; find out
where you sympathize rather than where you are
in antipathy, such is the spirit of Christ." Hence,
Count Tolstoi is reluctant to express opinions
upon controverted points, upon the authority of

the Scripture, upon miracles, and upon the familiar moot questions which are the battle-ground of fierce polemical debates. Speaking of human conceptions of God, he said : "What does it matter how we approach Him ? I approach Him by the metaphysical road. Yours is the road of the peasant ; it suits well the simplicity of the child. It is impossible to me. But why dispute ? All these roads are like the spokes of a wheel. They start from different points in the circumference, but they all meet in the centre."

But there are two points which Count Tolstoi would not regard as immaterial. The one is the conception of sin and its punishment, the other the Divinity of Christ. Sin, according to him, consists in conscious failure to abide in the will of God. All violence is sin. All participation in the fruit of violence is sin, for the receiver is as bad as the thief. If the Count takes money for any of his books, and that money has been stolen, he becomes a sinner equally with the thief. As the distribution of the goods of this life is based upon violence, we live in sin, encompassed by it constantly. We must try to live out of it by obeying Christ's laws. But sin is negative purely, and in reality is non-existent. Only the good is. The orthodox notion of Adam's fall and human depravity Count Tolstoi utterly repudiates. Still, he admits that in the soul, which is of God, there are imperfect elements, diabolic elements, which

lead it to choose evil rather than the truth. In
that choice lies the only judgment. The truth
would have made man free. He chooses falsehood,
and he is judged, for he remains in bondage, and
does not enter into the freedom which he might
otherwise have possessed. As for the idea of
other punishment for sin, that, he declared, was
contrary to reason. " Punishment and God are
antagonistic terms. God is love. The whole
idea of future punishment is radically false, and
contrary to the idea of God." I asked him how
he explained the parable of Lazarus. " Oh," said
he, promptly, " that is all wrong. It was spoken
in order to rebuke the social system which places
a yawning chasm between the rich and the poor,
and to satirize the idea very prevalent among the
rich, that the poor are their natural servants,
both in this world and the next. The moment
Dives sees Lazarus he expects that he will do his
bidding. The framework of the satire signifies
nothing. Christ constantly took the old Jewish
ideas and worked them into His parables. The
idea of judgment was archaic, it was not Christ's.
As for the vision in the Apocalypse, that was of
no authority." " But," said I, " what did Christ
mean when He said, ' Depart, ye cursed ' ? "

It was a very hot day ; we had had a long walk,
and Count Tolstoi changed the subject abruptly
by saying he was too tired to talk any longer.

The other point upon which Count Tolstoi in-

sists is the human character of Christ. Christ's
Divinity he recognizes in a sense. Christ spoke
the will of God, and he was God, for all of us
have what the peasants call a spark of God in the
breast. The great object of all religion is to develop that spark, to make man more divine. But
Christ was only a man like other men. The story
of His birth and of His resurrection seems to
Count Tolstoi purely mythical. He died, and He
did not rise again. He lived, He sinned, He
suffered, and He was crucified, rejoicing in His
ability to forgive in death those who injured Him.
Of the Atonement, he says it has had its day,
like torture, and disappears before the truer conception of the nature of God.

It is commonly believed that Count Tolstoi
denies the immortality of the soul. This is a
mistake. It is to him the best beloved of all his
speculative doctrines. We had many long talks
about the soul and the future life.

"Until two years ago," said he, " I thought but
little of the immortality of the soul. Now I think
of it constantly, and I ever think of it more and
more."

He believes in the free existence as well as the
immortality of the soul. Each soul had always
existed and would always exist. Nor would he
admit that the soul would not preserve its indi-
viduality.

"What is this ego? What is the soul? The

consciousness of being? It is not identity of matter. It is not identity of thought. It is like a string on which a continuous series of consciousnesses are strung. It is independent of the body. It will always be I. Life is a cone, cut at the apex by birth, and at the base by death. Existence is the continual broadening of the soul in love, which is the only true life, which is God."

"But," I objected, "there are souls which in life do not broaden, but shrink. What of them?"

"I cannot say," he replied, "for I know not what mysterious changes may take place at the moment of death, transforming a loveless nature. Or it is possible it may begin again a new existence on new conditions, in which it may have a new chance to fulfil the law of its being—which is love—which is God. It is with difficulty," he continued, "that I can tear my thoughts away from the next world. I regret every moment in which I do not feel that I am dying. If men could fully realize the truth and nature of the next world, there would be no keeping them in this. I long to depart. But this is wrong—I should be patient, and wait. Yet the thought of death is growing so increasingly pleasant that I need to struggle against the fascination of its approach."

It is interesting to be able to read Count Tolstoi's latest and most matured convictions on this subject, for hitherto most people have believed that he denied the immortality of the soul.

M. Anatole Leroy-Beaulieu, in his interesting study
of Count Tolstoi and religion in Russia,* says :

"Tolstoi denies categorically the future life.
In becoming Christian, he remains Nihilist.   He
admits for man no other immortality than that of
humanity.   According to him, true Christianity
knows no other.   Jesus, he says, always taught
the renunciation of personal life ; and the doctrine
of individual immortality, which affirms the per-
manence of personality, is in opposition to that
teaching.   The survival of the soul after death is
like the resurrection of the body—only a superstition opposed to the spirit of the Gospel."   This
may have been Count Tolstoi's opinion at one time.
It is not his opinion now.   " I will always be I," he
declares ; and the doctrine of personal immortality has assumed an importance in his conception
of life which is utterly at variance with the doctrines imputed to him on the strength of passages
in his earlier writings.   This change of front in
this important Christian doctrine more than
ever confirmed me in the opinion that Count
Tolstoi's religious ideas are still in the making.
This is to a certain extent admitted, even by
himself, nor is it probable that a thinker, who in
less than ten years has traversed the immense ex-
panse which separates absolute atheism, from a
Christianity of the very literal description out-

---

* Revue des Deux Mondes, Sept. 15, 1888, p. 434.

lined in " My Religion," can have already arrived
at finality.

Such is Mr. Stead's description of a portion of
his interview with Tolstoi. It seems very strange,
after reading of this remarkable man and having
been a student of his writings, to find one's-self
in his presence and to realize the different layers
of experience which were represented by this
remarkable life. As one looked into his face one
could see, according to the story as he himself
has given it in his Confession, the far-off student,
the dashing soldier of the Crimea, the society
man of St. Petersburg, the brilliant novelist of
later days, and last of all the arousing and awakened reformer of Russia, bearing his testimony to
the truth and righteousness of God, in the radical
and heroic manner of the old Jewish prophets.

The words of the Master came into the writer's
mind as together we walked over that far-off
plantation :

" And as they departed, Jesus began to say
unto the multitudes concerning John: What went
ye out into the wilderness to see ? A reed shaken
with the wind ?

" But what went ye out for to see ? A man
clothed in soft raiment ? Behold, they that wear
soft clothing are in king's houses.

" But what went ye out for to see ? A prophet ?
yea, I say unto you and more than a prophet. .

" And from the days of John the Baptist until

now the Kingdom of Heaven suffereth violence
and the violent take it by force. . . .

"He that hath ears to hear, let him hear."

The man seemed to be one part Quaker, like
George Fox, one part like a bit of Emerson and
another part a bit of the fanaticism of John Brown.
Again and again during this walk and conversation, one could not but be struck with the force
and power of the directly Christian literalism of
the man, going back as he did through creeds
and councils and the words of doctors and of men
to the direct commands of the Master.

"Why do you not organize, Count Tolstoi, and
gather your disciples around you?" was one of
the questions asked on this occasion.   "Ah,"
replied the Count, "life is different from organization.   Christ did not organize, he lived; let me
live, but let those that come after me organize.
It is the life which tells."   One thought of the disciples in the upper room at Jerusalem, who
organized after the disappearance of the Master.
One thought of Mohamed's followers organizing
after their great leader had died.   One thought of
the Lutherans in Germany organizing their church
after the death of their great leader; and it was
borne home upon the mind that in this matter
this man was both profound and wise.

"But," again was asked, "if you antagonize the
force of the government of Russia, in the way
that your friends fear, they may send you to

Siberia." "Yes," he answered as he played with a small, rough walking stick in his hand, "I may go to Siberia. I will probably be sent there at last and will die there, but it will be well; I will be happy to go." I looked at the man who uttered this sentiment. He was dressed in a moujik smock-frock with a waist-band as a girdle. He had on a woolen shirt whose collar was broad and ample. The grey hair of his head was long and silvery, and his iron-grey beard and moustache was silk-like and smooth, covering a tender, delicate and sensitive mouth. "Is Christ, indeed, your Master," I asked, "and do you think of Him as divine?" "Ah," he answered, "Christ brings me to the light. He may be God, he may be man, he may be both, but I see God only through him." "Have you published your principles to the world in the form of a creed?" was asked again. "No, no," he replied, "it is mine to have a few simple principles; so that the life tells. All the rest is unimportant." "What is it then," was asked, "which will make a life tell?" "Purity, humility, truth —these are the things which always make a man's life tell. I have not much to bequeath to the world," he added. "The banner of my life is self-abnegation." "Have you no faith in the churches as you know them?" was the next question. "Not as I see them," he answered. "The earth is the temple of the Lord and the churches hide themselves in an obscure corner of it. The Christianity of this nineteenth century," he added, "is a sham one. We must go back to the literal Christianity if we would indeed make the Gospel of Jesus a power." "What is it, then," was asked, "which corrupts men?" "War, society, government," was the prompt reply,—"it is these which corrupt men. To bring divine power again to man we must go back and back to the words and life of Christ."

"Do you believe, then," the writer asked, "in the progressive revelation of God to man?" "Certainly I do," was the reply. "If we occupy our minds with nonsense, however, God will never reveal himself to us. There will be no room for Him in our lives, but if we seek to do His will and live truly, it will not be a difficult thing to find God in our lives. The trouble is that too many of us are occupied with our nonsense and God can do nothing with a nature which occupies itself with nonsense." "Is there no hope then," was the next question, "for the Greek Church?" "None whatever," he replied, "though my dear friend Prince Ourouzeff would be shocked at my saying so. There is no hope for the Greek Church. It is a corpse; it is dead and nothing living can ever come from its tomb." "Ah, you must not think thus of all Christianity," the writer said. "Come and visit us in America

dead." "You are most kind," was the reply,
" and on some accounts I should like to go, but I
cannot now go to America. More must come
from my life and I must stay just where I am.
Man must not dissipate his life by travelling. If
his life is to be of any value he must live it out
and I must live my life out here."

At this point of the interview it seemed best to
drop the character of inquirer and answer the
many questions which seemed uppermost in this
man's mind.—Was our nation becoming frivolous?
Were the churches indeed alive? Had the reign
of dogma passed? Were the teachers and doctors of the Church going directly to the foundation
of all life in the words of Jesus? Were the
Shakers much thought of in America? Were
they not a harmless, innocent sect? Were the
Unitarians getting further from the word of
Christ or were they growing more into the spirit
of the Master? Was it possible for a man to be
truly liberal and yet be a member of the Anglican
Communion? Someone had sent him a volume
of the Rev. Phillips Brooks' sermons. Had I
ever heard the man, and did I know him? Someone else had sent him a book by a clergyman
in New York. It was called "The Right and
Wrong Uses of the Bible." Did I know the
author? Were the teachings of Henry George
thought well of in America? He himself thought
that George was an original and profound thinker,

and seemed pleased when I told him that we had
been boys together in my father's Sunday-school.
What kind of a place was Massachusetts? Would
they not think him very strange if he were to
visit America? He was afraid they might over-
power him with kindness; he had received so
many kind letters from America—ten letters from
America coming in the mail to one from England.
American authors he was most fond of, markedly
so of Thoreau, Emerson, Theodore Parker, Bry-
ant and Whittier. There was great danger
before the American people in the rapid growth
of luxury and wealth. Did we think the Republic
would avoid the mistakes of the republics of the
past?

At this point of the interview Prince Ourouzeff,
with his two companions, met us and in the dark
of the growing evening we entered the house
together and partook of a hospitable cup of tea
from the brass samovar upon the dining-room
table. As we passed a piano our host said:
" Play a waltz for the gentlemen, Leo; show
them how we amuse ourselves together," and the
music of the crackling fire upon the hearth kept
time to the bright waltz which Count Tolstoi
played for us, adding, "It is a waltz of my own
composition. I composed it years ago when I
was a society man in St. Petersburg."

By this time the sledges had come for us at the
door. Entering them we were kindly wrapped

up by our Russian friends and in the darkness of
that April evening we waved our farewell to the
Russian prophet and his pious host, and the
sleigh-bells jingled merrily as we struck the road
leading into Troitsa.

At Tavistock in Cornwall, on the 14th of June,
1889, the Honorable William E. Gladstone closed
an address before the electors with the following
sentence, which sentence lingers in my mind as
an emphatic realization of the influence throughout the world to-day of Count Leo Tolstoi :

"For character is moral power and moral
power it is which by the sure and unshaken
ordinances of God, working in ways perhaps unknown to us but known and fixed by Him and at
such times and in such manner as He shall
choose ; moral power it is which eventually
triumphs over every adversary and shapes the
fortunes of nations and determines the great
destinies of mankind."

CHAPTER XI.

In the treatment of Russian national literature we are dealing with a force that has been a living and continuous fact for nearly a century and a half ; and which has yet at least one great and commanding representative among the living writers of the empire.

Among the Russians, literature is no *dilettante* matter, but an affair as earnest as life, as solemn as death, and as real as nature. It constitutes no mere side-play, no idle resources of amusement ; with the educated classes, it is a fountain of inspiration that acts as a controlling force in life and is pursued with an intensity amounting to a veritable passion.

The spiritual energy of the Russian, with all the higher forces of his life, having been effectually excluded from the spheres of church and politics, is concentrated and intensified in the limited area of literary activity.

This is why the fire of the literary instinct burns with such peculiar 'brightness in Russia and shines afar with such undimmed and penetrating radiance : because it expresses the loftiest aspirations, the deepest purpose and the concentrated earnestness of a vast and masterful race. Energies which in other progressive nations are diffused over wide and varied fields, are here gathered up into one irresistible volume of passion, of thought, of love, of hate, of thwarted but determined purpose. In Russia, therefore, literature is the solitary medium by which the living current of divine prophetic fire and supernal inspiration reaches the national heart. It is the lever of progress, the engine by which heaven's forces are moving. For this reason, also, Russian literature has a national aspect and significance, such as no other but the Hebrew possesses.

The creator of Russian national literature was Michael Lomonosof. Out of the darkling chaos of primitive bilini, chronicles and ballad poetry, there sprang at his creative word a light for Russia whose growing splendor has been the masterlight of all her seeing ever since. He not only inaugurated the national literary era, but was obliged to create the literary language of his people ; and his services in shaping the form of the Russian language of to-day were greater than those of Chaucer in relation to the English tongue.

The life-story of Mikhail Vasilyevitch Lomonosof from his birth in 1711 to his death in 1765 reads like the veriest romance. His early life as the son of a fisherman and serf, roving about over the White Sea and the Arctic Ocean in the hard hunt for food; his enterprise in learning to read and write from the village priest; his stealing away from home to Moscow with a wagon train of frozen fish, in order to learn Latin; the favorable accident which placed him in a cloister school; his astonishing progress and subsequent brilliant career at Kieff and St. Petersburg; his travels and studies in Germany; his secret marriage and threatened imprisonment for debt, followed by his escape at the same time from the country and from a Prussian recruiting officer who had him entered in the cavalry service after getting him drunk; his marvellous success at St. Petersburg in science, in rhetoric, in poetry and in mosaic art—these facts bespeak the life of low-born genius and constitute a tale of adventure and achievement such as cannot be found in the life of any scholar, even of the Renaissance. Lomonosof left no monumental work of literary art behind him. In the province of literature he was simply a pioneer, the herald of a brighter day. He was a voluminous writer in the field of physical science, and devoted himself to many branches of it; proving himself everywhere a man of the most varied and profound learning. But his great work consisted in settling his native tongue as a vehicle for literary expression and in the new impulse which he gave to education and to the intellectual life of Russia.

Through Derzhavin and Zhukofski there is an unbroken succession of literary mediocrity from Lomonosof to Pushkin. It had been one of the distinguishing merits of Lomonosof's well-nigh universal genius that he was one of the noble patriots, almost fanatical in their aims, whose earnest toil intensified if it did not awake the sentiment of nationality in Russia. Yet all the poems of Lomonosof—constituting his distinctively literary work—were formed upon foreign models. Indeed it is characteristic of Russian genius that it lacks originality in the matter of literary form. And with the immediate successors of Lomonosof literary effort was a sickly imitation of the classicism after which his poetry was modelled, with the addition of a *dilettante* romanticism under the lead of Zhukofski.

The very list of the names of the writers and court-poets under Catherine II. is tedious and dull, like an interminable procession of black hearses with empty coffins in them.

Trediakofski, Sumarokoff, Kniazhnin, Kheraskoff, Bogdanovitch Khemnitzer, Viezin, Radistcheff, Novikoff—a dreary array of bombastic and artificial poetasters and wordmongers, with only here and there a momentary flash of spirited writing until, passing by the Alexandrine period of Kavanizin and Zhukofski, we reach in the reign of Nicholas, the great and honored name of Pushkin.

Alexander Sergeyvitch Pushkin was born at

Moscow in 1799, and perished in a duel at the early age of thirty-eight. With the opening of his brilliant career, Russian literature, passing out of its youthful stage attained its full majority, and entered upon its rightful heritage of independent freedom and power. It no longer bends beneath the yoke of the professional moralist nor serves as a medium for the inculcation of patriotism as blind obedience to the constituted order. It exists in its own right, standing erect and powerful, voicing and employing all the wild and native freedom of the human soul. Pushkin was the first among the memorable writers of Russia to grow restive under the political situation and to bid defiance to the prevailing despotism. For his keen satirical treatment of the ruling persons and conditions, including the idiotic censorship and the hated rule of the police, and for his bold defence of Shelley's atheism contained in an intercepted letter, he was twice exiled by the government— first to Southern Russia, whence he obtained leave to visit the Caucasus, there to fall under the influence of Byron's poetry; and lastly to his private estate for six years, where he escaped that inevitable participation in the revolt of 1825 which would have been visited with swift and certain execution.

Pushkin is emphatically the singer of the Slavic race. Yet even so patriotic a critic as Ivan Panim has denied him the rank of a true poet,

because he has no great controlling idea giving
force and harmonious unity to his work, but sings
merely under the ebullient impulse of a skill which
compels him to utterance. As a versifier he has
no peer; but his genius is wholly receptive and
artistic, never poetic or creative. He gives pleasure always but never imparts inspiration. He is
a worshipper of beauty for beauty's own sake and
a devotee of art for the sake of art. For this
reason the highest, the imperishable beauty
escaped him and the noblest art, the art that is
supreme because it is unconscious—lost in the
vision of the ideal—was beyond his grasp. This
aspect of his work was characteristic of the man,
and comports with the character of his mind and
life. His entire life, except the brief period of
his exile, was absorbed in the gay and voluptuous
high life of the capital. Spoiled in his youthful
education by French ideals and by a worldly
environment that had no redeeming feature, he
drowned his soul in the whirlpool of social vani-
ties and indulged even to his last days in the
silliest refinements of foppery. It is not wonderful, therefore, that in his works he neither
addresses the heart nor speaks from the heart.

Occasionally in his lyrical pieces, where Pushkin's art is always at its best, and toward the very
end of his brief life, in his finest prose work,
"The Captain's Daughter," he gives evidence of
a strength and depth of soul that was capable of

higher achievements. His "Hymn to Force" is one of the noblest and most beautiful of his lyrical efforts, but there is nothing distinctively Russian or strikingly original in it. It certainly reaches the highest region of poetic realization and sweeps the farthest horizon of scientific fact with infinite freedom and power ; but so far as regards its form and spirit it might have been written by Tennyson or Goethe or by our own Realf, whose unhonored genius soared as high as any that have ever sung.

Very different is the ringing note of the singing soul in his noblest poem, "The Prophet."

> "Tormented by the thirst for the Spirit
> I was dragging myself in a sombre desert
> And a six-winged seraph appeared
> Unto me on the parting of the roads.
> With fingers as light as a dream
>   He touched mine eyes ;
> And mine eyes opened wide,
> Like unto the eyes of a frightened eagle.
>   He touched mine ears,
> And they filled with din and singing.
> And I heard the tremblings of the heavens,
> And the flight of the angels' wings,
> And the creeping of the polyps in the sea.
> And the growth of the vine in the valley.
>   And he took hold of my lips
> And out he tore my sinful tongue
> With its empty and false speech.
> And the fang of the wise serpent
> Between my terrified lips he placed
>   With bloody hand.

And ope he cut my breast with a sword,
And out he took my trembling heart,
And a coal blazing with flame
He shoved into the open breast.
Like a corpse I lay in the desert;
And the voice of the Lord called unto me :
Arise, O prophet and guide, and listen—
Be thou filled with my will,
And going over land and sea,
Burn with the Word in the hearts of men."

Here the form and flavor are distinctly Russian. In this generation such a poem could not have been written out of Russia nor by other than a Russian hand. Elsewhere in this mammon-stricken time, there is no such " thirst for the Spirit " in the souls of men as drives them into desert solitude to be visited by six-winged angels of God ; the heavens do not tremble audibly in the ears of men in other lands, nor does the vine grow an audible message in any but Russian vales ; much less in this cant-cursed Western world is any sinful tongue torn out or a false and " trembling heart " replaced by the blazing flaming coal of the living Word. None but the semi-oriental spirit of the Slav impregnated still by the breath of truth and the eternal Spirit could possibly give birth to such an astonishing conception.

Pushkin perceived at the last, even through the mists of surrounding worldliness and inward variety, that art had a higher function than simply to entertain : that its aim was not pleasure but helpfulness. He saw clearly that its 'mission was the delivery of a message from the Infinite which must come out of the depths of the human soul ; but what that message was he never knew. He never would have known or guessed it. He had given himself over deliberately, knowingly, repeatedly into the toils of a constricting and consuming worldliness which crushed him and devoured him according to his deserts.*

In Michael Lermontof, the outward incidents of Pushkin's life were almost lived over again, whilst his spirit takes a step forward in that, with the intense Byronism of his works, he combines an uncompromising scorn for the brutal barbarity of the autocracy. Born at Moscow in 1814, he received the same type of youthful training which had forever shut out the soul of his great predecessor from the noblest destiny. He was twice banished to the Caucasus ; first at the age of twenty-three, for an elegy on Pushkin's death, in which he had the temerity to invoke the Czar's vengeance on the murderer who was a court favorite ; and again for a duel with a son of the French Minister Barante. Finally, at the age of twenty-seven, he was slain in a duel with a com-

---

* His principal works are the following : " Rusland and Sindmila," " Fountain of Bakhchisarai," " Prisoner of the Caucasus," " Lay of the Wiscoley," " Gypsies," " Ode to the Sea," " Boris Godunof," " The Captain's Daughter," " Eugene Ouyegin."

rade who had imagined himself insulted repeatedly, in Lermontof's romance, " The Hero of Our Time."

The inveterate vice of Lermontof, as of Pushkin, is the persistence with which he fixes his gaze upon himself and everlastingly describes himself and his own feelings in his works. From him we learn nothing of Russia. A spirit so subjective was incapable of holding the mirror up to nature and revealing the temper of his countrymen and the condition of the land and time in which he lived. His redeeming excellence is that he was too brave and true ever to compromise with the evil which he hated and denounced. To the last he refused to fall down and worship the golden image. In his own proud words : " They tortured him because he dared to think ; stoned him because he dared to speak ; they could make no answer and that was the sole cause of their frenzy. " " But he did not envy them nor their servility by which they were won. They robbed him of everything except his pride and courage. He was on fire for the beautiful, fought for the true. The others found that to be bad and dangerous. When liberty is taken from him long, solitary contemplation changed his hate to boundless contempt."

In him we see the awful tremblings of those new forces that were beginning to stir in the heart of Russia ; we hear the stern protest

against that autocratic brutality which has turned
Russian history into one long tragedy of more
than fifty years—a protest that swelled to more
majestic and terrible tones in the literary epoch
that immediately followed, and which has determined the character and direction of literary
development in Russia ever since.

With the appearance of Nikolai Vasilyevitch
Gogol (1809-1852), Russian literature passed
finally beyond the subjective romanticism that
had ruled from Zhukofski to Lermontof, and not
only entered on a new epoch, but opened a new
era in the world of letters. Gogol is a realist of
the most original and impressive type. A native
of the steppes of southern Russia he grew up
amid the wild and radiant beauty of a luxuriant
and expansive nature ; whilst his inheritance of
Cossack freedom and daring familiarized him
with the untamed life and rude simplicity of that
most original people. His heart was tutored to
sincerity and his imagination inspired by the tales
of adventurous heroism recounted at the home
fireside.

At the age of twelve he entered school at
Nyezhin, where he was voted a dunce under the
humorous sobriquet of Universus Mundus—the
first words of the opening paragraph in a Latin
Reader, which paragraph measured the extent of
his progress into the mysteries of the Latin
tongue. With like stupidity in mathematics he

abhorred it equally with the classics; nevertheless he read voraciously, established a college review with himself as chief contributor and took the town by storm with his acting in the amateur theatricals which he inaugurated. At twenty years he was off to St. Petersburg, having outgrown the provincial horizon, and filled with hunger for the companionship and fame of Zhukofski and Pushkin.

Here, after all manner of tribulation, penury, starvation, disappointment ; after failure successively as a government clerk, university lecturer, and on the stage ; and after having gone off to Germany, to Lubeck, in the vain pursuit of fortune, he finally resolved to devote himself to the literary life, come whatever fortune would. Hereupon, he straightway enters upon a career of imperishable renown as a writer. In 1830 he began a series of tales entitled " Evenings on a Farm," portraying the wild life of Cossackdom in colors of such beauty and with scenes of such thrilling interest as at once enchained the heart of the nation. One of these, " Taras Bulba," takes rank in Russia as a national epic and is praised by Russian critics of high authority in terms of most extravagant laudation, as worthy of comparison only with the Iliad. It is unquestionably a tale of unique power, in which the whole Cossack nature speaks, unfolding all the heroic qualities and strange life in the ancient Cossack republic.

Another tale much admired by Western critics is "The Cloak," detailing the petty miseries of an ill-paid government clerk, who all his life has wanted a Spanish cloak and has the long-coveted garment stolen from him shortly after becoming its possessor.

It is not as a teller of stories, however strong or fascinating, that Gogol reaches his high standard in the field of literature. This he attains in the sphere of practical moral purpose, as a conscious and caustic protester against the shameless abuses of the autocracy. His first attempt in this direction was by the path of the drama in a comedy entitled "The Revisor," or Government Inspector. His professed aim was to drag into light " all that was bad in Russia " and wither it in the fire of indignant scorn.

He laid bare the abuses and corruption of the civil service with a biting satire and placed the alternate arrogance and servility of the officials in a light so ridiculous that it aroused universal contempt for the official class and at the same time evoked their instant and bitter hostility. The guilty officials of a small city, whose administration will not bear investigation, dreading the advent of a secret examiner who, they learn, has been sent from St. Petersburg on an errand of investigation, call in a body at the hotel where he is supposed to lodge, and there mistake a penniless spendthrift traveller for the dreaded inquisitor,

He, after momentary surprise, accepts the situation when he sees them bent on warding off his condemnation by the methods common to corrupt officials. He accepts all their bribes; borrows money on all hands ; makes love to sundry maids and matrons, including the mayor's wife and daughter; and finally disappears with all his booty, to be succeeded by the real revisor to the utter dismay of the officials who, secure, as they supposed, in the Revisor's favor, had launched forth upon a new career of outrage. Such is the plot of this famous play. The delicate subject was handled with such artistic skill under the bewitching veil of impersonal humor which disguised the author's indignation, that the censorship scarcely hesitated to allow its presentation, and the Emperor Nicholas, at its first performance called the author to him and said : "I have never laughed before as I have this evening." To which Gogol replied, "I had really aimed at another effect."

This moral end sought and aimed at in "The Revisor," was fully attained in Gogol's great novel, "Dead Souls," which was directed against the abuses of serfdom. An audacious adventurer goes about Russia making fictitious purchases of "Dead Souls," *i. e.* of serfs who have died since the last census, yet who were still counted as living, intending to people with these nominal beings a worthless tract of land with a view of pledging all to the government by means of ignorant and corrupt bank officials.

This flimsy plot, which is scarce intelligible to a Western mind, but which was vividly understood by every Russian of the time, is simply an excuse for painting the dark aspects of Russian civilization—or rather barbarism—and for introducing numerous types of Russian society. It is a sort of panorama of Russian life. It revealed Russia to the Russians and made them realize how little they·had felt the awful sores which were poisoning the life-blood of the empire. " Great God," exclaimed Pushkin, on reading it, " I had no idea Russia was such a dark country ! "

In these two great works "The Revisor" and " Dead Souls," Gogol transcended the narrow limitations and barbaric ideals to which he had been born, as well as the traditional romanticism of the time and launched forth upon a hitherto unexplored sea, demonstrated with marvellous skill and amazing genius that conscience and moral purpose could be made a commanding force in literature. It was he that emancipated literature from the thraldom of an artificial tradition and led it forth from the world of dreams into the atmosphere of real life.

His life ended sorrowfully enough. Finding that his genius had exhausted itself in the work of protest against the crying evils of his native land, and was incapable of constructive or idealizing achievement, he burnt the second part of "Dead Souls," on which he had labored long, as unworthy his best art, and giving all his possessions to the poor, he devoted himself to a religious life.

Wishing to make a pilgrimage to Jerusalem, he published a volume of private correspondence to obtain the needed funds for the journey and drew down upon himself a storm of denunciation from his former liberal associates for the spirit of Christian submissiveness and humility exemplified and commended in these letters. He was mercilessly abused as an imbecile and a renegade ; and, heart-broken at the coldness or hostility of former friends, took refuge in the most extreme religious mysticism. Giving himself over to fast and vigil, that wrecked his mind and wasted his body, he was at last found starved to death before a shrine, in front of which he had been prostrate in silent prayer. So passed from labor and from suffering the noblest, most original, and most striking figure in the field of Russian literature, and one who, for purity of soul, elevation of purpose and Christliness of spirit, is without a peer in the universal republic of letters.

The closing years of Gogol's life witnessed the appearance of a body of clever and accomplished writers who won a national recognition—Shevtchenko, Byelinski, Niekrasof, Herzin, Tchrunishevski, etc.—whose names are scarcely known

out-side of Russia and who contributed hardly
anything distinctive to the national literature.

With the rise of Ivan Turgenief we reach a
period and a man in Russian literature that are
both imposing and familiar to the entire reading
public in every Western land ; for his cosmopolitan
genius and Russian spirit made Russian literature popular in the West and prepared the way
for his younger contemporary, Tolstoi.

Rarely indeed has an author obtained a triumph
against such terrible odds as did Turgenief.   He
has been read and admired in every land where
art and genius win the homage of mankind ; but
never, outside his own land, has he been read in
his own tongue.   Everywhere his work has become known through the medium of translations ;
yet even when thus distorted and robbed of its
finest finish, his work has everywhere elicited the
most genuine enthusiasm and commanded the
highest respect.

The style of a great author is the quality and
feature of his work which always makes the most
effective impression—the vehicle on which his art
is carried to the goal of the reader's appreciation ;
yet Turgenief's style is almost wholly unknown
to the bulk of his readers, and his art is
made real to them through the style of the trans-
lator.   That in spite of such obstacles his art
should have made its way during his own lifetime
into the unqualified admiration of the civilized

world is more than ample proof of its excellence. It was the supremacy of his literary art that enabled him to conquer universal recognition. There is an architectural symmetry and completeness of form in every one of his books not to be found so perfectly exemplified in any other modern author. In this particular each of his six great novels is a perfect masterpiece. Nothing is superfluous ; yet nothing is wanting. No three-volume standard compels prolixity and endless verbiage ; no commercial tyranny of the bookseller drives the author to disregard nature and perspective whilst pandering to the popular whim of the hour. In fact, there is no such thing known in Russia as bookmaking. The author is before all things an artist with the most exacting standards and the most conscientious regard for the demands of his art. Hence, in Russia there are few scribblers but many writers, who have produced few volumes but have executed many masterpieces.

One supreme virtue of Turgenief's art which makes his work thrill and glow under the eye of the reader like a thing of life and beauty, is his deep sympathy with nature. There was in his soul that unconscious poetic discernment of the living force that animates the world which made him reverent toward nature, in spite of his agnosticism, and led him to paint the universe as a living thing. The air trembles under his eyes, the sunshine laughs, the thunder growls as he listens ;

even the darkness is clothed with intelligence and feeling, and the warmth of a summer eve is charged with a message of peace, as in this exquisite sentence from one of his minor stories: " Night, silent caressing night, lay on the hills and dales. From its fragrant depths afar—whether from heaven or from earth could not be told—there poured a soft and quiet warmth."

Above all Turgenief has the rare dramatic power of living in the characters which he creates, and so of making them live and breathe before us. He himself was conscious of this power as he said to Mikhailof, Professor of Physiology in St Petersburg : " I see a man who strikes me from some characteristic or other perhaps of little importance. I forget him. And then, long after, the man suddenly starts up from the grave of forgetfulness. About the characteristic which I observed others group themselves, and it is of no use now if I want to forget him : I cannot do it ; he has taken possession of me ; I think with him, live in him ; I can only restore myself to ease by finding an existence for him."

The weak aspect of Turgenief's work was not on the artistic, but on the moral side. He was a man utterly devoid of faith : hence, there is nothing positive or inspiring in his purposes. The pall of an immovable pessimism hangs over all his work. Melancholy, dark, stubborn, impenetrable, possesses him. Whatever purpose rules his work—and his art is full of purpose—is negative, critical. He is a fighter, a destroyer. The Russian autocracy that shadowed his youth and blighted his manhood, making him a hopeless exile, was the foe that called out the energy of his nature in life-long hostility.

Pushkin stood for the expression of literary independence; Gogol for that of satirical protest and earnest criticism; in Turgenief we reach the attitude of determined assault and persistent enmity to the existing social order—the literature of pure negation and destruction, if not of despair.

With the work of Dostoyevski we begin to ascend toward a new order. There is in the strange, complex, incomprehensible nature of this marvellous man, a boundless prophecy of positive constructive genius which never gets its fulfilment. He never gets beyond the analytic stage. But it is a distinct and immeasurable gain over all that preceded him in Russian writing that he is analytical, not critical; dialetic, not cynical; psychological, not sociologic or economic in his view of man and human relations. Here, at last, we feel that we are dealing with the primordial elements out of which all social fabrics are constructed, namely with those human instincts and motives which are the source of all maladjustments of social relation and organization. The conditions and activities of the human soul are the engros-

sing matters of his interest. Outward nature
makes no impression on him. There are no land-
scapes in his background ; no descriptions en-
cumber his pages. But with a perfectly clairvoy-
ant perception of mental conditions and spiritual
processes, he opens up dark continents of undis-
covered thought and motive, traversed by streams
of action and consequence, and embracing impenetrable jungles of problem and mystery. "Crime
and Punishment" is an analysis of motive and an
unfolding of spiritual sequence unsurpassed, if not
unequalled, in any language ; and makes one feel
how slight and trivial in comparison is such a psy-
chologic portrait as "Dr. Jekyll and Mr. Hyde."
Apparently the simple analysis of a special crime,
it is, in reality, a vast picture of the psychology
of contemporary Russia, with its social conditions
for background. With little or no art employed
in its structure and with many vices of style, the
story is yet enthralling by virtue of its intense
realism and profound tragic verity.

In his sympathy with the human soul and in
his immediate and clear perceptions of its laws
Dostoyevski is the true forerunner of the great
personality who claims the main story of this
volume.

ℓ

THE CZAR AND HIS FAMILY.

CHAPTER XII.

THE night train from Troitsa hurried the travellers back that same evening to Moscow, refreshment having been secured at intervals along the way. The note-books were much in use that night in making entries of this interesting day's work, and the sleep of the just crowned the night with its blessing in the comfortable Hotel de Berlin, in Moscow.

The next day saw these same three pilgrims going once more over the sights of the Kremlin and through St. Savior's massive structure, to the house of the Tolstoi family to report the success of their visit to Troitsa. On the way thither a family group of the Tolstoi children, with Miss Tatiana, the elder sister, and the English governess, were discovered walking to see the rise in the river Moskva, which was bounding along like a New England river in a spring freshet. After giving the children an account of our visit to their father and Prince Ourouzeff, which conversation was instantly translated into Russian by the elder sister, Miss Tolstoi added : " Ah ! yes, you see they are great cronies, Papa and Ourouzeff, and

they don't agree one bit ; but they are fast friends."
And the happy group of children went running
along to see the river, waving a farewell to the
Americans, who turned once more to see that
never-failing object of interest, the Kremlin, with
its many souvenirs of the past. Along the river
side many peasants were occupied in getting that
familiar harbinger of spring, the always welcomed
"pussy-willows." Groups of peasants would secure for themselves little branches of these, which
were tied together with colored ribbons, and
would then proceed to the different shrines and
icons in the churches within the Kremlin walls,
there to dedicate them to their favorite saint and
patron.

As we re-entered the Troitski or Trinity Gate of
the Kremlin—the gate through which Napoleon
both entered and left Moscow—a curious sight
met our eyes. A detachment of gray-coated soldiers was being reviewed by the officer in command,
whereupon a conversation ensued in Russian between the commander on horseback and the troops
who were drawn up in line ; which conversation
was translated to us by our guide as follows :

(Officer in command.)   "Soldiers, are you
well ?"

(Soldiers giving a salute.)   "Yes."

(Officer in command.)   "Soldiers, are you ready
to suffer ?"

(Soldiers giving a second salute.)   "Yes."

(Officer in command.) "Soldiers, are you
pledged to defend your country?"

(Soldiers giving a third salute.) "Yes."

Hereupon the commanding officer, giving in
return a salute, left the detachment which had, in
the meantime, grounded its arms, and went over
to a second detachment to go through this military catechism with them.

Murray says of the Kremlin that "Russian ar-
chæologists are unable to trace the name to any
certain source. It is by most supposed to be derived from the Russian word Kremen or silex, but
it occurs for the first time in its present form in
the year 1446.

"Originally part of the site now occupied by it
was enclosed by walls of oak. Demetrius of the
Don, laid the foundation of stone walls in 1367,
which resisted the Tartars on several occasions,
and were only seized by Toktamysh through
treachery. In 1445 the Kremlin was burned, and
the walls and gates partly destroyed. The introduction of artillery rendered the old walls, although
repaired, no longer safe against invaders. John
III. invited Italians to build new fortifications of
stone, which were accordingly erected between
the years of 1485 and 1492, and subsequently extended and strengthened. These walls alone
escaped the ravages of a fire that destroyed the
whole of the Kremlin in 1737. They are now
7,280 feet in circumference and pierced by five

gates, the principal of which, the Spaski or 'Redeemer' Gate, nearest the Church of St. Basil, was
built by Peter Solarius, a Milanese, in 1491. Christopher Galloway, an English clock-maker, built
the tower in 1626, and placed a clock in it which
was, however, later replaced by another. Hence
the style of the tower is Gothic, and out of keeping with the Italian battlements : it is the Porta
Sacra and Porta Triumphalis of Moscow. Over
it is a picture of the Redeemer of Smolensk, held
in high veneration by the Orthodox. An omis-
sion to uncover the head while passing under this
gate, was anciently punishable by fifty compulsory
prostrations. The traveller should not fail to pay
the respect to old traditions here exacted, since
the Emperor himself conforms to the custom.
Criminals executed in front of this gate, offered
their last prayers on earth to the image of the
Redeemer of Smolensk, which also witnessed the
execution of the Streltsi by Peter the Great. In
his reign the sectaries who refused to shave their
beards paid a fine in passing through this gate.

"The next gate in importance alongside the
Spaski Vorota is the Nikolsky or Nicholas Gate.
The miraculous image of St. Nicholas the Mojaisk,
'the dread of perjurers and the comforter of suffering humanity,' is suspended over it. Oaths
were anciently administered to litigants in front
of this venerated image. The tower was originally
built in 1491 by an Italian architect, but has, like

the other buildings of the Kremlin, been restored
after successive disasters. The troops of Tokh-
tamysh, of Sigismund III., and of Napoleon passed
through this gate within four centuries. In 1408
it witnessed the siege of Moscow by Edigei ; in
1551 the invasion by the Crim Tartars ; and in
1611-12, the battles between the Poles and the
Russians for the possession of Holy Moscow. It
was, also, partly destroyed by orders of Napoleon,
when it escaped with only a rent which split the
tower in the middle as far as the frame of the
picture but not even the glass of the picture ; that
of the lamp suspended before it was said to have
been injured. An inscription to that effect was
placed over the gate by order of Alexander I.

"A gate near the western extremity of the
Kremlin wall, is called the Troitski or Trinity
Gate. Its tower was likewise built by Christopher
Galloway in the early part of the seventeenth
century ; restored in 1759, and after the conflagration in 1812. The French both entered and
left the Kremlin by this gate. Before that invasion the buildings in the vicinity afforded a refuge
for vagrants, thieves and murderers, who kept the
inhabitants in great terror."

After a farewell sight of the Church of the
Assumption where a great service was being held
with a musical refrain which sounded like a chorus of the colored Jubilee singers, and after another survey of the Church of the Annunciation,

where the Czar is always crowned, we turned from tombs of the Romanoff princes with the tomb of Ivan the Terrible built as an annex just outside the church, and went to the banker's for rouble notes enough to carry us out of Russia.

"Where have you come from?" asked the polite, man-of-the-world young man. "We have come from Troitsa," was the reply.

"What took you to Troitsa?" he inquired once again.

"We went to see Count Tolstoi," was the answer.

"Count Tolstoi?" inquired the clerk in an incredulous tone of voice, "well, have you seen the big bell in the Kremlin—the Tsar Kodokol or King of Bells?" The reply was in the affirmative.

"Well, then if you have seen the big bell of Moscow, and Count Tolstoi," replied the clerk, "you have seen the two objects of interest; and the same thing has happened to each of them— *they are both cracked!*"

Such was the Russian verdict upon our pious pilgrimage to Troitsa; and there the conversation at the banking office ceased.

The happy thought generally comes too late. When seated in the cars an hour later the right answer came to this remark. "Yes," should have been the reply, "but in such a God-forsaken, darkened country as Russia one rejoices in the light which comes in even through a crack."

The route from Moscow to Warsaw is almost

the identical route taken by Napoleon on his retreat from Russia. The cannon which surround
the gates and walls of the Kremlin, with the proud
letter N stamped upon them, are the only remaining souvenirs of the French occupancy of this
sacred shrine of the Russian people.

Borodino, the river Beresina, and the smoky
town of Smolensk, were passed on the journey,
while the imagination was busy in conjuring up
the facts of history all along the memorable and
historic route.

"On the 23d of June, 1812, the French crossed
the Niemen and pushed on to Wilna, the Russians
carefully retreating and leaving Napoleon to pass
that river on the 28th, and enter the town unop-
posed. Here the French emperor remained
eighteen days, and then, after considerable man-
œuvering, marched on to Vitepsk, where he fully
expected to bring the Russians, under Barclay de
Tolly, to action. The Russian general, however,
declined ; and Napoleon instead of following the
advice of his marshals and wintering on the Dwina,
crossed the Dnieper and marched on Smolensk.
On the 16th of August he was once more in front
of the Russian grand army near that town ; but
the wary and intelligent de Tolly had occupied it
only to cover the flight of its inhabitants, and
carry off or destroy its magazines ; and on the
following morning Napoleon, to his great mortifi-
cation, learned that the enemy in pursuance of his

Fabian tactics, was again off.   Smolensk was now taken by assault, the last inhabitants that remained having set fire to it before they left.

"Up to this time the Russian commander-in-chief had been able to adhere to his plan of drawing the French into the country without risking a general engagement until a favorable opportunity should occur—tactics which were not liked by his army, and Alexander, yielding to the clamor, appointed Kutusoff to the command.

"The battle of Borodino, sometimes called that of the Moskva, fought on the 1st of September, was the result of this change of leaders. The combatants amounted on either side to about 120,-000, and the killed and wounded in both to about 80,000.   On the 12th, Bonaparte again moved forward, his troops by this time nearly famished and heartily tired of the war, for the day of Borodino had given them a clear idea that the enemy would only yield after a desperate struggle.   On Sunday, the 13th, the Russian army marched out of the old capital, with silent drums and colors furled, by the Kolomna Gate, and left the city to its fate. In the afternoon of Monday, the advanced guard of the French army caught the first view of her golden minarets and starry domes, and the Kremlin burst upon their sight.

"'All this is yours,' cried Napoleon, when he first gazed upon the goal of his ambition, and a shout of 'Moscow! Moscow!' was taken up by

the foremost ranks and carried to the rear of his
army. In Moscow they bivouacked the same
evening. Ere the night had closed in, their leader
arrived at the Smolensko Gate and then learnt, to
his astonishment, that 300,000, inhabitants had
fled and that the only Russians who remained in
the city were the convicts who had been liberated
from the jails, a few of the rabble, and those who
were unable to leave it. On Tuesday, the 15th
of September, the mortified victor entered Moscow and took up his residence in the Kremlin;
but here his stay was destined to be short indeed,
for on the morning of the 16th it was discovered
that a fire, which had at first given but little
cause for alarm, could not be restrained—fanned
by the wind it spread rapidly, and consumed the
best portion of the city. 'The churches,' says
Labaume,' though covered with iron and lead,
were destroyed, and with them those graceful
steeples which we had seen the night before re-
splendent in the setting sun; the hospitals, too,
which contained more than 20,000 wounded, soon
began to burn—a harrowing and dreadful spectacle—and almost all these poor wretches perished,
a few who still survived were seen crawling, half-
burnt, amongst the smoking ruins, while others
were groaning under heaps of dead bodies, en-
deavoring in vain to extricate themselves. The
confusion and tumult which ensued when the
work of pillage began, cannot be conceived.

Soldiers, sutlers, galley-slaves and prostitutes were seen running through the streets, penetrating into the deserted palaces, and carrying away everything that could gratify their avarice. Some clothed themselves in rich stuffs, silks and costly furs, others dressed themselves in women's pelisses ; and even the galley-slaves concealed their rags under the most splendid court-dresses ; the rest crowded to the cellars, and, forcing open the doors, drank the wine and carried off an immense booty. This horrible pillage was not confined to the deserted houses alone, but extended to the few which were inhabited, and soon the eagerness and wantonness of the plunderers caused devastations which almost equalled those occasioned by the conflagration.' 'Palaces and temples,' writes Karamzin, 'monuments of art and miracles of luxury, the remains of past ages and those which had been the creation of yesterday, the tombs of ancestors and the nursery cradles of the present generation, were all indiscriminately destroyed ; nothing was left of Moscow save the remembrance of the city, and the deep resolution to avenge its fate.'

"On the 20th, Napoleon returned to the Kremlin from the Palace of Petrofsky, to which he had retired, and soon tried to negotiate with Kutusoff, who replied that no treaty could be entered into so long as a foreigner remained within the frontier. The Emperor then requested that he would forward a letter to Alexander. 'I will do that,' said the Russian general, ' provided the word *peace* is not in the letter.'

" To a third proposition, Kutusoff replied that it was not the time to treat or enter into an armistice, as the Russians were just about to open the campaign. At length, on the 19th of October, after a stay of thirty-four days, Napoleon left Moscow with his army, consisting of 120,000 men and 550 pieces of cannon, a vast amount of plunder, and a countless host of camp-followers. And now the picture of the advance was to be reversed. Murat was defeated at Malo-Yaroslavets on the 24th, and an unsuccessful stand was made at Viasma on the 3d of November. On the 6th, a winter, peculiarly early and severe even for Russia, set in. The thermometer sank eighteen degrees, the wind blew furiously, and the soldiers, vainly struggling with the eddying snow, which drove against them with the violence of a whirlwind, could no longer distinguish their road, and falling into the ditches by the side, there found a grave. Others crawled on, badly clothed, with nothing to eat or drink, frost-bitten, and groaning with pain. Discipline disappeared, the soldier no longer obeyed his officer ; disbanded, the troops spread themselves right and left in search of food, and as the horses fell, fought for their mangled carcasses, and devoured them raw ; many remained by the dying embers of the bivouac fires, and as these expired, an insensibility crept over them, which soon became the sleep of death. On the 9th of November Napoleon reached Smolensk, and remained till the 15th, when he set out for Krasnoe. From this time, to the 26th and 27th, when the French crossed the Beresina, all was utter and hopeless confusion ; and in the passage of that river, the wretched remnant of their once powerful army was nearly annihilated. The exact extent of their loss was never known, but a Russian account states that 36,000 bodies were found in the river alone, and burnt after the thaw. On the 5th of December Napoleon deserted the survivors ; on the 10th he reached Warsaw, and on the night of the 18th, his capital and the Tuileries. The army that had so well and enthusiastically served him, was disposed of as follows :

Slain in fight	125,000
Died from fatigue, hunger, and the severity of the climate	132,000
Prisoners	193,000
	450,000

"The remains of the grand army which escaped the general wreck (independently of the two auxiliary armies of Austria and Prussia, which knew little of the horrors of the retreat) was about 40,000 men, of whom it is said scarcely 10,000 were Frenchmen. Thus ended the greatest military catastrophe that ever befell an army in either ancient or modern times.

" To return to Napoleon. Europe was now exasperated and combined against him, and though, in the following spring, he gained the battles of Lutzen and Bautzen, and on the 27th of August, that of Dresden, fortune deserted him on the 18th of October of the same year, on the field of Leipsic. On the Rhine the allies offered him peace and the Empire of France, which he refused, and on the 31th of March, 1814, Alexander had the satisfaction of marching into Paris."

As the train came to a halt at the station at Smolensk, and was delayed for awhile in the matter of some freight or baggage, the following particulars as regards this city on the Dnieper, were taken from a Russian source :

" When the grand army began its march from the Niemen, in 1812, the Russian troops fell back on Smolensk. Although Barclay de Tolly encouraged the inhabitants and assured them of their safety, he nevertheless caused the treasury to be removed, and all documents from which the enemy might derive any information about the condition of the country. The two Russian armies (one commanded by Barclay de Tolly, the other by Bagration) reached Smolensk on the 22d of July (O.S.) and encamped on the left bank of the Dnieper. Three days later they retreated further, leaving only one regiment in the town. In the meanwhile the French advanced, and, after the engagement with Neverofski at Krasnoi, appeared

on the 3rd of August in the neighborhood of
Smolensk. Raefski, sent to assist Neverofski, for-
tified as far as he could, the suburbs of the town,
and resolved to maintain himself in it until the
arrival of the two armies.

" On the morning of the 4th (16th) of August, the
fighting commenced, and was continued the next
day with great carnage, as the armies had advanced
the day before. Many assaults were repulsed, the
old walls withstood a fearful cannonade, and a
dreadful fire broke out in the town. . . . .
During the night our troops evacuated the town,
and on the morning of the 6th (18th) Napoleon
entered it, but found nothing but smouldering
ruins, and no inhabitants except the old, the
young, and the sick, many of whom had taken
refuge in the churches. Napoleon remained four
days at Smolensk, and established a Commission
for the civil administration of the town, with Cau-
laincourt as Military Governor. The Commission
could, however, do nothing ; a rising took place
all over the country ; bands of partisans were
formed, and destroyed foraging parties, and even
larger bodies of the enemy, whenever they met
them. The French tried to overawe the people
by acts of severity, and, having seized the leaders
of two bands of partisans, Engelhard and Shubin,
shot them, at Smolensk. This only increased the
animosity of the people, and when, on the 29th of
October (O. S.), Napoleon returned to Smolensk,

he found nothing for the support of the remnants
of the ' great army.'

" The further retreat of Napoleon was protected
at Smolensk by Ney, who left the city on the 6th
(18th) of November, after blowing up eight of the
towers built by Godunof ; and a part of the other
fortifications. The Russians who had remained
in the town, issued out of their places of refuge,
and began to destroy with frenzy the stragglers
who roamed about the town, throwing them
into the flames of the burning buildings, and into
holes in the ice.

" The Twentieth Regiment of Rifles entered
Smolensk and put an end to these outrages. The
removal and destruction of the bodies of men and
carcasses of horses, were continued for three
months afterwards ; for many of the streets were
literally encumbered with the dead.

" At first, the bodies were burned, piled in heaps
half a verst in length and two fathoms high ; and
when the supply of wood failed, they were buried
in trenches and covered with quicklime. Epi-
demics subsequently broke out in consequence.

" The losses incurred by Smolensk were at that
time valued at 6,592,404 r. 60 c.

" The mounds which cover the bodies of the unfortunate Frenchmen will be seen on either side
of the old post-road from Moscow.

" Although the demolition of the historical walls
of Smolensk has been commenced by the town

council, there is reason to hope that this act of vandalism will go no further ; and that the traveller passing through the old city will still catch a glimpse of its ancient defences."

The train upon which we were travelling in this forty-four hour journey out of Russia, consisted of nineteen cars and two engines, with heavy well-ballasted sleeping-cars.

A party of opera singers belonging to the Royal Opera Company of Berlin, were upon the train, having come up to Moscow from Odessa and the Crimea on their way back to Berlin.

There were some Norwegian and Swedish singers in the party, and one tall, splendid looking man in the company found his way into our compartment, being attracted thither by the jolly voice of Lord Byron, who was singing some gentle snatches from " Mikado."

" Pray go on," said this professional basso. " I like to hear other people sing—I, too, am a singer."

In vain Lord Byron protested his inability to sing before a professional : the neighboring female singers were sent for and in a little while our compartment was crowded with an admiring and not over-critical audience, the ladies smoking Russian cigarettes and applauding the unknown English words of Gilbert and Sullivan's favorite opera.

Through Minsk and Ledletz and other Polish

towns this overland train slowly but effectively
plodded on its way, along a dreary country unin-
teresting in the extreme in its physical aspect,
and over-flooded with the spring freshets of April,
as its history had been flooded with the blood of
the thousands slain in the Russian and Polish
wars and uprisings in the past.

A curious episode on this exit from Russia was
found in the fact that our unknown basso friend
proved to us, then and there, that after all, this
earth of ours is a very little world.

In giving us his impressions of the Wagner
school of opera, in a very modest and intelligent
way, he mentioned the great tenor, Nieman, who
had recently rendered the Wagner trilogy in New
York. One of the party having mentioned that
he himself was at the Metropolitan Opera House
in New York, on the night when Nieman made
his debut as Siegfried, added—" But after all that
is said about Nieman in " Die Walkure," I preferred the " Hunding " who appeared with him that
evening; he was even greater than Nieman."
" Oh, thank you, thank you, gentlemen!" exclaimed our basso friend, making a profound bow.
" You have very much complimented me—I was
" Hunding " that night."

There was not very much to see in the old
Polish city of Warsaw. Thaddeus of that place
was dead, and we knew of no other character half
so interesting. I believe we stayed in the build-

ing—now used as a hotel—where Napoleon stopped when on his flight from Russia. But we did not have so much upon our minds as he had, and did not leave our baggage and things on the way, as his custom was.

A little later on, we stopped at the same hotel at which, on a former occasion, the Grand Duke Don John, of Austria, the hero of the naval battle of Lepanto, as described in Motley's " History of the Dutch Republic," stayed ; but this far-off fact of history made no appreciable difference in our appetite or sleep or manner of life.

A miserable Polish commissionaire tried in vain by the help of the most detestable French, to cheat Mr. Thackeray out of two five-rouble notes —but was balked of his nefarious purpose by the bold and continuous appeal of Lord Byron and the other member of the party to the "Chef de Police," which appeal they kept murmuring in soft and liquid cadences—now rising, now falling like the rhymthic sequences of the Greek chorus— appealing to the gods for vindication ! The sleeping-car conductor on this same Russian train, a Pole, who used execrable French, tried a bluff game upon these innocents, forbidding them the use of their apartments on some technical ground ; hoping thereby to extort a bribe from each of these strangers—whereupon Lord Byron and his friend resorted again to the Greek chorus appeal to the Immortals in the likeness of the helmeted and be-buttoned police.

These two short but effective episodes impressed upon the minds of the travellers the fact that, after all, there was a good deal to be said in behalf of the partition of Poland, and that if " Freedom shrieked when Kosciusco fell," it might be as the writer once heard a certain minister begin a funeral discourse—that Freedom, like the orator on the occasion, " was not intimately acquainted with the deceased."

At five o'clock on the morning of April 15th, at Sasnowice, on the frontier, our passports were asked' for, and after a short inspection they were returned to us on German soil again.

We could have embraced the German custom-house officers, so glad were we to see their familiar uniforms again ; and at Breslau, at ten o'clock, we breakfasted on the old German roll again, and took the train for Dresden.

The electric ding-dong bell of the well-known Dresden Stadt sounded four o'clock in the afternoon as the travellers emerged from their railway carriages at the Dresden depot.

The run through Russia had been made, it was no fool's errand after all. Each member of the party said his good-bye, and entering his carriage, drove off.

Russia and Tolstoi had been seen and had been conquered—and " every man went unto his own

www.ingramcontent.com/pod-product-compliance
Lightning Source LLC
Chambersburg PA
CBHW021436020726
47499CB00006BA/2031